MEIKYUU: LABYRINTH KINGDOM
A TACTICAL FANTASY WORLD SURVIVAL GUIDE

Iori Miyazawa

ILLUSTRATION BY Yo Shimizu
ORIGINAL WORK BY Toichiro Kawashima
AND Adventure Planning Service

A maze of stone and lumber stretched as far as the eye could see.
To my right, to my left, and above and below.
"A world entirely engulfed in a labyrinth—
we call this place **Million Dungeon**."

Mizuho the Frequent
Late-Nighter

Taiga Andou-Garrett

Troach of the
Complicated Past

"I, Astoria, am on a journey in search of adventure.
I shall gladly accept your kingdom's invitation!"

Astoria the Wing-Blessed

MEIKYUU LABYRINTH KINGDOM

(A TACTICAL FANTASY WORLD SURVIVAL GUIDE)

Iori Miyazawa

ILLUSTRATED BY
Yo Shimizu

ORIGINAL WORK BY
Toichiro Kawashima

AND
Adventure Planning Service

YEN
ON

New York

MEIKYUU LABYRINTH KINGDOM
(A TACTICAL FANTASY WORLD SURVIVAL GUIDE)

Translation by Alice Prowse ("Popo")
Cover art by Yo Shimizu

MEIKYUU KINGDOM TOKUSHUBUTAI'SAS' NO OSSAN NO ISEKAI DUNGEON SURVIVAL MANUAL Vol. 1
©Toichiro Kawashima 2019
©Adventure Planning Service 2019
©Iori Miyazawa 2019
First published in Japan in 2019 by KADOKAWA CORPORATION, Tokyo.
English translation rights arranged with KADOKAWA CORPORATION, Tokyo through TUTTLE-MORI AGENCY, INC., Tokyo.

English translation © 2021 by Yen Press, LLC

Yen On
150 West 30th Street, 19th Floor
New York, NY 10001

Visit us at yenpress.com ◊ facebook.com/yenpress ◊ twitter.com/yenpress ◊ yenpress.tumblr.com ◊ instagram.com/yenpress

First Yen On Edition: August 2021

Yen On is an imprint of Yen Press, LLC.
The Yen On name and logo are trademarks of Yen Press, LLC.

Library of Congress Cataloging-in-Publication Data
Names: Miyazawa, Iori, author. | Shimizu, Yo, illustrator. | Kawashima, Toichiro, author. | Prowse, Alice, translator.
Title: Meikyuu, labyrinth kingdom, a tactical fantasy world survival guide / Iori Miyazawa ; illustration by Yo Shimizu ; original work by Toichiro Kawashima, Adventure Planning Service ; translation by Alice Prowse.
Other titles: Meikyuu kingdom: tokushubutai SAS no ossan no isekai dungeon survival manual. English
Description: First Yen On edition. | New York : Yen On, 2021–
Identifiers: LCCN 2021025590 | ISBN 9781975325121 (v. 1 ; trade paperback)
Subjects: LCGFT: Light novels. | Science fiction. | Fantasy fiction.
Classification: LCC PL873.195 M4513 2021 | DDC 895.6/36—dc23
LC record available at https://lccn.loc.gov/2021025590

ISBNs: 978-1-9753-2512-1 (paperback)
       978-1-9753-2513-8 (ebook)

10 9 8 7 6 5 4 3 2 1

LSC-C

Printed in the United States of America

index

Chapters

1

Twelve hours and forty minutes after being stuffed into economy class on a British Airways flight from Heathrow to Haneda, I finally arrived in Japan.

After crossing the boarding bridge and arriving inside the terminal, I stretched to loosen up my body, which had stiffened from the long flight. My scapulae cracked.

A long line of Japanese people returning home had formed at the immigration inspection booth. I passed by them without stopping, queuing for foreigner immigration.

Ahead of me was a financier from the UK who had started talking business over the phone before even entering the country, a pair of mothers wearing hijabs while pleasantly chatting in Arabic with children in tow, and a young Indian man who didn't glance up from the video on his tablet for even a moment. When at last all of them had been processed, my turn came. The immigration inspector looked at me, then made a slightly dubious expression.

"Hello," I said to the man, handing him my passport. The name on it read Taiga Andou-Garrett. Nationality: the United Kingdom of Great Britain and Northern Ireland. Essentially, it meant I was Japanese-British.

"What's the purpose of your visit?" he asked me in English.

"On my way home," I responded in Japanese, grinning like an idiot. "I was born in Japan."

At that, the inspector finally switched to Japanese as well. "Where in Japan?"

"Kawasaki."

The inspector flipped through my passport's pages, a complex look on his face. He scanned me up and down a couple of times, not hiding the suspicion in his eyes. Objectively speaking, I probably did look dubious. My features didn't betray any immediate ethnicity, and everyone told me that I was terrible at giving an insincere-but-friendly Japanese smile.

"You've certainly been around, haven't you?"

"Yes, on work."

"What do you do?"

"Military."

"What?"

"I used to be a soldier. Just resigned recently, though."

The inspector still seemed to have his doubts, but eventually, he stamped the passport and gave it back to me with an unamused gaze.

"Thank you," I said, bowing my head slightly before taking my passport and heading past immigration. I got nervous at passport control every time, despite not having anything in particular to hide. I'd entered other countries aside from Japan and the UK with false identification during operations before, and I thought of those experiences even when I went somewhere with the proper paperwork. I wouldn't need to give immigration a carefully doctored profile for myself anymore. I'd simply come back to the country where I was born and raised.

Now, most passengers would be waiting a little while for their luggage to come around on the turnstile, but all I had was my rucksack. I passed the baggage-claim area and went through an automatic one-way door leading to the entrance lobby.

Immediately, a crowd of people holding up welcome signs written in multiple languages—OKAERINASAI, HUANYING GUANGLIN, WELCOME TO JAPAN—all focused their eyes on me for a moment before realizing I wasn't who they were here for and looking away. Without drawing anyone's attention, I joined the crowd of people moving every which way through the lobby.

There was nobody to greet me upon my return. I hadn't lied about going home, but that didn't mean I had any relatives. My stay was more of a grave visitation. It had been a long time since I was last in Japan; I'd returned once ten years ago for my mother's funeral. The terminal was a lot tidier than I remembered it being. It seemed to me there were more foreigners, too—me being one of them now.

Wondering whether to take the train, monorail, bus, or taxi home, I headed for the food court. I had to fortify myself with some food first.

At a window-side seat, I ate a bowl of *tsukimi*—egg-yolk-topped—tempura soba and watched the passenger jets taxi down the runway one by one.

After finishing the noodles, I sipped at some black tea I'd bought at another stall. The stuff had become a staple of mine since being thrown into the British Army at sixteen. Amazingly, I'd seldom had any while I lived in Japan, but now, after a military life of twenty years, I was all but addicted. Those guys really did drink this stuff anywhere. In tanks, in the jungles of Southeast Asia, in the deserts of Arabia... I'd consumed it right alongside them, too, to the point where I could say without much doubt that black tea composed a significant portion of the molecules making up my body.

It was two PM. No one was waiting for me, but I wanted to get to Kawasaki before dusk. Once the sun set, the temple gates would be closed.

After that, I had no plan. My resigning from the military, an institution I'd spent most of my life in, had been a turning point. Thus, I figured visiting my homeland was a fair first step since I hadn't done so in a while.

Well, I'm here now, so maybe I'll go on a sightseeing trip around Japan.

I did have the savings for it. Plenty of time, too. I was unemployed, after all.

Yet even that wasn't something I was gung ho over. I only came to it by process of elimination. In truth, I wanted to work, to have a job somewhere that made use of my skills.

As I continued sipping my now-lukewarm tea, I perked up.

Someone was watching me.

Pretty much anyone who had been through a good amount of training would agree that people like us knew when we were being watched. We could sense their presence, feel the weight of eyes glued to our backs. Detecting such a thing was even easier when the watcher meant us harm. And the gaze on me was filled to the brim with murderous intent.

I held my smartphone to my ear, pretending to be on a phone call as I glanced over to the mirrored wall. I'd initially chosen a seat where I'd be able to watch my own back. For an instant, I saw a hooded figure in black among the throngs going back and forth; they abruptly crouched. It was a casual gesture, one easily explained as them tying a shoelace.

Still, after waiting a bit, I recognized that this person in black didn't get back up. I'd found my observer.

Continuing my feigned conversation, I got up from my seat and started walking. I didn't know who they were, but that hostility could only mean one thing. Someone was after me. Trying to kill me, a former SAS soldier.

2

SAS stood for the Special Air Service, a British special-forces unit that was the greatest in the world in both name and substance. Those in it didn't call the organization the SAS, however; just "the Regiment."

Until a month ago, I'd been one of them.

Calling it the best wasn't out of bias or conceit. It was a simple fact. The selection tests to get into the Regiment were the harshest in the world, and even those who failed earned praise for having made an attempt. The level of training you received upon admission was globally considered the most excellent as well. Peacekeeping forces from every allied nation would come to us to learn from our skills. Ever since its formation on the Arabian Peninsula in World War II, it had seen plenty of actual combat. We'd be secretly deployed to shady places at home and abroad to do our jobs efficiently and go home. It was a band of professional warriors—taciturn, vulgar, sweaty, and loyal to their own.

It was comforting to exist in that world since it contained only professionals, but being part of that sort of thing for so long made it easy to forget that most people weren't that way. Every once in a while, you'd happen upon a complete idiot who forced you to remember that such types still existed. Sometimes, folk like that could ruin all sorts of things for you. In fact, one such moron was the reason for my discharge.

It all started in Ankara, the capital of Turkey. I'd falsified my identity to gain entrance to the country for an operation, which I proceeded with carefully. I can't say much about it, but my mission was to set up a "conversation" with a high-ranking military official who we were almost positive was in contact with a certain foreign power. With help from a local collaborator familiar with the region, I established a plan, and I was all ready to carry it out the following day.

Then that associate leaked a photograph of me.

Either the guy was trying to distract himself from his anxiety, or he was stoned—but whatever the case, he took a selfie in the café that night, with the caption *With a friend from the SAS!!* followed by a bunch of emoticons, then uploaded it to Instagram. I was behind him; he covered me up with a sticker, but some nearby window glass, polished to a sheen, caught my reflection perfectly.

It boggled the mind to think anyone could have done something so foolish in the middle of a mission.

I caught word the next morning and was understandably furious. Sadly, there was nothing I could do. After immediately reporting the incident to my superiors, the mission was called off. They ordered me to withdraw; I was out of Turkey within four hours.

Though I returned home safely, I was in an awkward position. Operatives in the Regiment worked on highly secretive missions, and we needed to avoid having our faces revealed. Look at any book or article about the SAS—the hard rule about public photographs was to blur out the head. More than a few people had a bone to pick with the SAS. Any identifiable members were in immediate danger.

Frontline work was no longer an option for me. My superiors offered me the choice of taking on rear support operations, but I wanted to stay in active service.

The whole thing was unfair, but the responsibility lay with me. I obviously didn't have a good eye for people, and I hadn't noticed the picture being taken. The mission had failed, and my comrades ended up having to clean up after me. Try though I did to help, there was no longer anything I could do.

I couldn't afford to stay in the Regiment any longer. Thus, I'd resigned from the military after twenty years of service.

Several old friends and acquaintances who heard about my plight had offered to let me stay with them. There were many job opportunities, too—private-military-company operative, weapons-company observer, combat instructor... There was even an offer from a publishing agent wanting to know if I'd write a book. To top it all off, and I don't know how they heard about me, but a big entertainment-promotion company even e-mailed me to see if I wanted a namesake TV program. Everyone loved those shows where former special-forces agents had to survive in extreme environments. I was assured the ratings would be phenomenal.

Even after leaving the SAS, its shadow continued to loom over me. I'd have no worries about being able to fill my belly for the moment, at least, and I was grateful for the many offers. Yet the only response I gave was that I'd consider the propositions and respond later.

To be perfectly honest, I was hurting. I had been reborn in the Regiment and had lived my life there. The SAS had been my *world*, and I was deeply shocked when I had to leave it against my will. No matter how pleasant the conditions in my new workplace would be, regardless of pay, that pain wasn't the sort that mended quickly.

And so I had decided to be a vagabond for a little while until my frayed nerves calmed. The first step on that trail was here in Japan.

There was another reason I hadn't started my next job right away.

Now that my face was public, I knew that some who were less than friendly toward me would be watching. This wasn't a persecution complex. Imagine how big a problem it would cause for the British government if a terrorist organization were to kidnap a former SAS member and hold him hostage. Ponder on how much top secret intel could be wrung from me if a foreign spy were to catch me in a honeypot. I wouldn't be taken in so easily, of course, but there was nothing saying that enemies wouldn't try.

Me departing the UK and wandering was also so I could keep an eye on my general vicinity and wait for things to blow over. A few years after leaving active service, my value as an asset to those villains would drop dramatically.

Such had been the plan anyway...

I was surprised—I hadn't thought someone would be after me right from the outset. Turkey, Afghanistan, South Africa, Thailand... There were stacks of grudges. Still, this one had come to collect sooner than I'd expected.

I pretended to hang up and returned the smartphone to my pocket. I'd check on the tail again, decide between leaving the area and taking control, then execute—just like I had done so many times in the past. Now that someone was glaring bullets into my back as I walked through the airport, the only thing on my mind was how to deal with this situation.

3

Crossing the international terminal, I kept an eye on my new shadow. As I went through the crowds and bought some magazines and stationery at various shops, I would switch directions as though I'd changed my mind, then check a guide map and look around to "try and get my bearings."

I spent about twenty minutes on this observation task, but it looked like I only had a single tail. Their black hood kept jumping in and out of sight, denying me a good look at their face. However, there was definitely something unnatural about their movements compared with the rest of the people around.

This is strange, I thought. It reeked of amateurish work. Typically, you tailed someone as part of a team. This person might have been the bait to draw my attention away from the others, but they were still incredibly artless about it.

Then again, if this *was* an absolute layman, that presented its own troubles. Without the tacit understanding of what they would do if they were a professional, I had no idea of when and how they'd move in.

I directed my gaze upward and checked the surveillance cameras that were all throughout the building. Airport security was tight. No matter what you did or where, they'd have video evidence. Even with such recordings, assassinations and terrorist attacks still occurred. The person who had used nerve gas to kill Kim Jong-nam, a North Korean, at the Kuala Lumpur International Airport a few years ago had been an average Indonesian woman.

The Kuala Lumpur incident was the sort where people had used a throwaway assassin to carry out the attack, and professionals had been observing from a safe place. Still, as far as I could see, nobody was giving my hooded follower instructions. I went up escalators and elevators, too, to check other places they might be watching from, but nobody stood out. Either this person was alone, or they had drones or something keeping a constant eye on me...

Now that my face was public knowledge, maybe it was best to assume there was a bounty on my head on the dark web. This could even be an amateur assassin, given only a photograph of the target and their flight name, coming after me for a pittance. Their intentions were unclear, but if they were going to use bombs or gas, it could lead to unwarranted collateral damage.

I turned away from the center of the terminal and continued in the least-populated direction I could find. I sped up slightly to try and make my pursuer impatient. If they really were acting solo, they would have to follow at my pace.

Continuing, I walked into a restroom at the terminal's edge—the only place in the airport without any cameras.

If this follower wanted to kill me, this was their perfect chance, and it served me well, too. In this situation, the presence of security cameras was actually disadvantageous for me. I wanted to live a life that didn't involve getting arrested for excessive self-defense.

Upon entering the empty restroom, I made a tight tube out of the magazine I'd bought at a shop and quickly wrapped it with tape. Then I set down my rucksack and plunged my hand into it, retrieving a Sure-Fire flashlight. A makeshift club made from a rolled periodical and a flashlight were the only weapons at my disposal. I had no gun or blade.

It might have seemed silly to those convinced that SAS soldiers were cold, unfeeling killers, but the thing we really excelled at was acting safely and in secret. Sure, it might be easy to simply kill a hostile encountered during an operation, but if it caused a whole lot more trouble in return, what would be the point?

After assessing a threat level, we did what we could to avoid such an option.

Only when necessary did the options to attack, flee, or kill come into play.

Hurried footsteps approached, then came into the restroom. The hooded figure stopped when they saw me ready and waiting. I turned on the SureFire in my left hand. Strobing it quickly, I succeeded in causing my assailant to cover their face with an arm reflexively. This flashlight was strong enough to block out a person's vision and induce dizziness. I closed the distance, then whacked my pursuer's throat through their hood with my magazine club.

They grunted and collapsed. Still, it didn't feel like I'd struck them especially powerfully. From the sensation, I would've guessed they had a scarf around their neck. Deciding to take control before my opponent had a chance to regroup, I moved to grab the person's hood.

No sooner had I tried than I heard a door open behind me.

Immediately, I turned around just as another figure was coming out of a stall farther into the restroom. *Impossible*, I thought. I would have noticed someone in there when I entered.

This new combatant didn't have a human face. The man wore a black suit, and on his face was a grotesque mask that looked like a moray eel— large eyes, and a row of fangs sticking out of the mouth.

The first person staggered to their feet. Their hood fell off. This one's disguise resembled the head of a white crow, with a sharp beak and eyes the color of blood.

Two thugs wearing animal masks. They still hadn't drawn weapons. After warding the moray eel off with the strobe light, I jumped at the crow, grabbed his facade, and tried to twist it to the side. The disguise couldn't allow him much of a field of vision, so a slight shift would completely block his view. To my surprise, however, the beak opened and let fly a shrieking caw. Even I couldn't help but be surprised. My hand clutched not at a rubber mask, but an ample layer of down. I saw my stunned expression reflected in the surface of the creature's glossy eyes.

Regardless of the plausibility, this was the living head of a ridiculously large albino crow. The bird-man lanced forth a white-gloved hand, and the next thing I knew, I was in the air. Such monstrous strength from such a slender body. My back slammed into the tile, knocking the wind out of me. The flashlight left my hand, and my magazine-club soared away.

The eel and the crow looked down at me from above; then, in synchronous movements that spoke of practice, they pulled long, straight-bladed swords from nowhere. Nothing I had seen thus far suggested they'd been carrying weapons of that size.

Suddenly, the lights in the restroom went out.

The two man-beasts shouted something, sounding disturbed, but I'd never heard their language before. Not wanting to let the opportunity escape, I groped around for the flashlight I'd dropped and eventually grasped it. As I tried to get up, I realized there was a faint red light surrounding me. I looked down to see, hovering just above the floor, a circular pattern. It was twisting and gnarled, looking like a maze. The design rapidly expanded until it covered the whole floor. I found my gaze drawn to it—as though my eyes had started searching for the maze's exit without me telling them to.

A light clattering started up—and then came quakes strong enough to knock me off my feet.

It was an earthquake, a big one. The force was so great that I couldn't stand. On all fours, I checked how my enemies were doing. The eel and the crow had blended into the dark; I couldn't see them. Had the terrible shaking not demanded my attention, I would have pondered that curiosity longer. I'd never experienced tremors like this. Undoubtedly, there would be a lot of casualties... The floor danced, the walls warped, the support beams bent, and the ceiling split, letting in incredible sounds from every direction. Puzzlingly, I couldn't *see* anything. It was too dark to have been a typical power outage. Despite it being the afternoon, no light spilled into the restroom from outside.

All at once, the floor under me opened. *I'm going to fall!* I immediately cradled my head in my arms and rolled myself into a ball. The crashing and cracking of the building collapsing accompanied me as I plummeted into the darkness.

Cold water caught me.

It wasn't very deep. My hand met the gritty stone at the bottom. I paddled to get my head above water. Switching my SureFire off its strobe mode, I cast its light around. The eel and the crow were nowhere to be found.

When I stood up, I found that the water was only knee-deep. Attempting to get a handle on the situation, I wheeled the flashlight around to get a better picture. Unfortunately, the sights hardly cleared anything up for me.

I was in what looked like a stone passageway. The walls and ceiling both had cracks in them, moss grew in large tufts, and water flowed steadily along the floor. It was an old-looking chamber—almost like ruins.

A cave-in had blocked off one end. Had the earthquake caused it to collapse? I checked the ceiling with my light, but the hole I was sure I'd fallen through was nowhere to be seen.

As my light passed over the caved-in section, I stopped dead in my tracks. A young woman was collapsed on the ground. She was half submerged in the water and lay still. Either she was dead or unconscious. Her long hair bobbed and swayed with the gentle stream. It was also a curious shade: vivid blue.

4

"Hey—"

My call echoed unexpectedly down the passage. I watched and waited for a few seconds but saw no signs of anyone reacting to it.

I approached the woman. She was slumped against a large piece of debris, but a cursory examination revealed she wasn't grievously wounded.

Squatting down next to her, I brought my ear close to her mouth and nose.

She was breathing.

"Can you hear me? Can you answer me?"

"Uff..."

After addressing her again, her eyelids began to twitch, and she let out a soft groan, but nothing more. It seemed she was temporarily unconscious.

I carefully parted her hair and checked for any external head wounds. The locks were blue right down to the roots. So then this had to be her natural color. It was baffling, but I set it aside for now.

As I prodded at the skin of her head, I felt a slight elasticity. She seemed to have a little bump. No blood or fluids were leaking from her ears or nose. I used my fingers to lift an eyelid and shine my light into her eye, which contracted. This was normal pupil reaction. Her left eye didn't show a significant difference in size from her right, either, meaning there was no evident brain damage. If the swelling on her head was the cause of her unconsciousness, then it couldn't have been more than a slight concussion.

She was still soaking in cold water from her waist down, so I decided to bring her up on top of the debris after checking the footing. Otherwise, she would have quickly gotten hypothermia.

As gingerly as I could while remaining wary of possible fractures or dislocations, I picked her up under my arm and pulled her out of the water. Her face was white, and her lips were purple. Admittedly, I was soaked and feeling cold myself. We needed to get somewhere warm, and quick, or we'd be in danger.

I was one thing, but she was in more trouble. Wearing soaking-wet clothes while unconscious would continue to sap her of body heat. I wondered if I should remove her garments for now—any awkward predicaments when she awoke were something I hoped she understood the reason for—but no, even if I did, I had nothing to warm her with. Nothing to start a fire, and no dry clothing. Besides—

I glanced again at the outfit she was wearing. All it took was a glance to recognize how strange it was. From the roughness of the fabric to the detailed embroidery, it didn't quite seem like something from the twenty-first century. What to call it? It wasn't like a toga from ancient Greece, nor was it a monk's robe. Colorful, decorative pieces of cloth adorned her shoulders and skirt, suggesting some sort of religious motif. However, her limbs were wrapped with material to protect her joints, and she wore well-used gloves and boots over them.

I knew there were people in the world who spent a large part of their lives participating in historical reenactments and video-game cosplays, but this was the real deal. There were minor stains and smudges, her sleeve hems were a bit frayed, and patchings and mendings stood out in a few places. It all looked, for lack of a better term, *lifelike*. Persuasive enough to make me think she wore this regularly.

The young woman's features were odd, too. Her skin was paler than any I'd seen, and she had large eyes. Her build was on the short and slender side as well. On the whole, the blue-haired girl looked childish. I'd seen many different ethnicities, people, and cultures, but she matched none of them.

Who was this person? Where was she from? Some had found my mixed Japanese and British features strange before, too, so I was in no position to judge.

As I wondered what to do, the woman groaned and stirred. She had regained consciousness at last.

"Are you all right? Don't move too quickly. Open your eyes slowly—"

Finally, my words seemed to reach her brain. Her eyelids snapped open, and her eyes focused. After seeing me, she sat up, seeming panicked.

"*Awka! Hek twey pa? Neupa pooluf?*"

"Umm." Those were not words I understood at all. "Uhh, *konnichi wa? Hallo? Nihao? Marhaba? Shalom?*"

As I was listing off all the greetings I knew, an expression of surprise slowly crept over her face.

"*Oh tangara! Hek yarha rahassa!*"

"What language is that? Errr…"

"*Rak Shanto? Rak Hyperboa? Rak Oars?*"

"I'm sorry, I have no idea—"

"*Rak* Earth?"

I blinked. That last word sounded to my ears very much like natural Japanese.

The woman, perhaps gauging my reaction, emphatically continued. "Earth? You, yes, came, Earth, yes? *Niet?*"

Was I being asked if I came from Earth? She was making it sound like this was some other planet.

Questions swirled in my mind, but this blue-haired girl was waiting wide-eyed for my reply. Reluctantly, I opened my mouth to speak.

"Yes…but—"

"*Oh tangara!*" she cried out, standing up. Just as I wondered if it was okay for her to do that so quickly, she unsurprisingly staggered.

"Whoa there."

I reached out to support her, but she seemed too excited to care.

"You, yes, came, Earth, person! You, *Visitor!*"

The last word had a clear emphasis, and the blue-haired young woman pointed at me as she spoke it.

"Visitor?" I repeated.

My inquiry prompted her to nod forcefully. "You, stay."

Saying it as though giving a dog a command, she reached for her hip. Hanging from the clasps on her belt were several pouches and bags. She unhooked one of them, then unraveled the string tied tightly around the opening. Her hands seemed very used to the motion. Out came a feather about the length of a finger. It was bright and vivid, a gradient of red, gold, and green, reminding me of a tropical bird.

She brought the feather up to my nose. I tried to pull away from the ticklish feeling, but she made an intimidating "shh" sound to stop me.

"You, *niet*, go. Yes?"

She seemed to be telling me not to move. I didn't know what kind of magic trick I was in for, but not seeing many alternatives, I acquiesced. The blue-haired girl nodded, her face serious, then continued tickling my nose with the feather.

What was going on?

The plume had a smell like coriander. Unable to process the situation, I wondered when I should stop her, the itchiness climbing up my nostrils. Sparks flashed behind my eyes. I immediately considered, in all seriousness, if this was some kind of mean-spirited drug—when from an unexplored region far behind my nose that I hadn't even realized was there before now, a violent urge to sneeze crashed over me.

"Hah... Hah...hah... *Achoo!*"

The extra-large blast of air exploded out of me—and in that same instant, a huge bird squirmed through my nose and mouth and burst outside.

"What the—?"

I stared wide-eyed at the creature, which didn't even turn back. It flapped its wings, then grabbed the feather the woman was holding in its mouth and disappeared into the darkness.

"What was that?! What did you just do?!"

"Oh, good. It must have worked."

The girl's voice sounded relieved, which made me even more confounded.

"What did?! Did a bird just come out of my—?"

"It's okay. Just calm down. It was a Babel bird. That's what they do."

I couldn't remember being this panicked for at least a decade. The shock was so great that it took me a few moments to realize we were able to converse now.

Finally catching on, I stopped my wailing. "...Did I just understand you?"

"Yes, Mr. Visitor."

"Why now?"

"Because I used the down of a Babel bird. It was precious, something I inherited from my great-great-great-great grandmother. I'm so glad it worked."

"A Babel bird...?"

"There's a legend saying that this method works with Visitors who come from Earth. Apparently, you're *supposed* to understand the words from the beginning, but a bird nests in your head that prevents you from comprehending."

"My head? A bird? Nesting?"

"Yes, in between your ears, far behind your nose," she stated plainly, washing her hands in the running water. I must have sneezed on her hands.

I rubbed my face with both hands in disbelief. I could still feel the bird's body scraping against my nose hairs. I couldn't even imagine how that thing had come out of me.

After she washed her hands, she stood up.

"I am Mizuho the Frequent Late-Nighter. What is your name, Visitor?"

"I'm, er...Taiga. Taiga Andou-Garrett."

"And what is your title, Taiga?"

"My title?" Did she mean that epithet after her name? "No title. Just Taiga. Where am I anyway?" I asked, dazed.

Mizuho answered, "This is not the Earth you were in before, Taiga."

"It isn't...?"

"This is a world entirely engulfed in a labyrinth—filled with terrible monsters, ancient magic, and perilous traps. We call this place Million Dungeon."

Million Dungeon—as those words sunk deep into my head, emptied as it was after chasing the Babel bird out, my feet started to shake a little.

Another earthquake.

5

The tremors swiftly grew more intense. Waves formed in the waterway, and dust began to fall from the ceiling. With a sharp noise, a crack formed in a wall.

Immediately, I pulled Mizuho close.

"Wah…!"

"Get down. Cover your head," I instructed, covering her with my body and using my other arm to protect my own skull. No suitable egress presented itself, so it was all we could to do hunker down and wait for the rumbling to subside.

With a sound that sent a shiver down my spine, the ceiling collapsed. A chunk of boulder fell right where Mizuho had been passed out. The water's surface raged like a school of fish was excitedly swimming through it, sending cold sprays at me.

Gradually, the shaking subsided until, eventually, it was quiet.

"Looks like it's over. Are you all right?"

"Y-yes!"

I released Mizuho and got up; she bounded to her feet like a spring.

"Thank you so much!"

"Hmm?"

"You saved me, did you not? I just remembered that I was unconscious before."

"Oh, right."

"I'm sorry. This is my first time meeting a real-life Visitor, so I got excited…"

"I didn't do anything. You woke up on your own; that's all. More importantly—"

"Oh, I forgot! My glasses!"

Suddenly getting flustered, Mizuho started searching all around her. Before long, she spotted the cylindrical case, opened it, and breathed a sigh of relief.

"Thank goodness. I have bad eyes, so I can't live without these," she admitted, taking the spectacles out of the case and donning them. As she looked at me through them, they had gold rims and elaborate decorations, she blinked, momentarily taken aback.

"Something wrong?"

"Oh! No, I, umm. You have a sterner face than I expected..."

I cocked an eyebrow.

That seemed to snap her out of it. "I-I'm sorry! From what I heard, Visitors are younger—like handsome rosy-cheeked young men in uniform, or energetic girls with short hair and bushy eyebrows. I'm a little disappointed—or rather, surprised, and—"

"Well, sorry for being old enough to be your uncle. Anyway, I had a question—"

"Yes! What is it? You can ask me anything!" she responded, breathing heavily through her nose.

Flustered, I managed to continue, "Er... You called this place Million Dungeon, right? Are earthquakes common around here?"

"Earth-quake?" repeated Mizuho, seeming confused.

Come on, I thought. We were speaking so normally to each other—why would the word *earthquake* be the exception?

"Like how the ground was rumbling before—"

"Oh, so on Earth, you call them Earth-quakes!"

"Uh... Yeah."

Mizuho produced a small stone slab out of nowhere and took a loud, scratching note on it with a stylus before looking up again and saying, "About that! We call them dungeonstorms!"

She was very excited.

"Dungeonstorms...?"

"Yes! Storms occur from time to time here in Million Dungeon. It messes up rooms, breaks apart corridors, mixes up floors, and squashes monsters and people alike. They're awful things. I got caught in one, and the next thing I knew, I was here—"

Mizuho's words suddenly cut off.

"What is it?" I pressed, growing impatient.

Seeming somewhat lost, Mizuho said, "Where are we?"

"Huh?"

"Um, that's right, I...," she muttered, rubbing the bump on her head. "I was in the room and heard a loud noise... Then the wall turned up, and the floor slanted... And after that..."

Mizuho shut her eyes tight—did she have a headache? She seemed ready to stagger and fall over again, so I put a hand on her elbow to steady her.

"Don't push yourself. Take slow breaths."

Mizuho opened her eyes, looked at me, and said, "Taiga! I have to go back to my country!"

"Your country? Where is it?"

"I don't know..."

"What's it called?"

"Support Roman Empire Post Five."

What?

"...You have Rome here? Nearby?"

"Romes aren't that unusual. I know of at least ten nations with that name."

"I see."

I stopped thinking about it. I didn't have a clue how our communication worked despite us speaking entirely different languages, but the translation engine—or whatever was behind it—was probably malfunctioning. It had to be.

I looked down at Mizuho; she was upset to the point where her previous enthusiasm seemed like a dream. Her gaze was unfocused, the color had left her face, and she was having trouble standing. She'd maintained her momentum because of her wound-induced adrenaline surge and her conversation with me, but their effectiveness was wearing thin. Her wet clothes were leeching her body heat. Whether or not the young woman realized it, she was exhausted.

I snapped my fingers in front of her face to draw her attention. "Mizuho. Let's find the way back. Help me."

"Ah... Right, right!"

"Good. First, we'll move somewhere safe. We don't know when this passage will cave in. Let's find somewhere secure and open. Understand?"

"An open...space..." Mizuho made a complicated face at that, but I continued anyway.

"Once we find a good spot, we'll make a fire. We're both soaking wet. We'll dry our clothes, rest a while, and have some tea."

"Tea?"

"If only we had some food... Did you bring any?"

"Unfortunately, no..."

"I see. In that case, we'll just have to make do."

"You have tea?"

"Not with me, but I should be able to find some soon. Can you move?"

"I'll be fine."

"All right. Let's get moving."

Mizuho and I set off in search of a haven.

6

With one end of the passage blocked by collapsed stone, there was only one direction we could move. The path along the shallow waterway was just barely big enough for two to walk side by side. I took the lead, lighting our way with the flashlight and having Mizuho follow a few meters behind. The passage sloped slightly in the direction we proceeded in, but it continued to be straight. A draft blew from up ahead. That implied an open space was this way, but it also meant my soaked clothing would get colder and colder.

There were several rules when it came to survival situations. Most of them had been made into acronyms. (The military had many such abbreviations. I figured it was because the terminology was overly long to begin with.)

Different instructors had their own ways of imparting the same things, but the basics didn't change. The first thing I learned was the abbreviation PRWF.

P stood for *protection*—to protect yourself.

R stood for *rescue*—to put yourself in a place where help could find you.

W was for *water*—to secure water.

F was *food*—to secure food.

In a survival situation—that is, in any circumstance where your life was at risk—anyone could panic and lose sight of what to do. So long as you recalled those initials, you'd at least know the essential priorities.

The four rules of PRWF were listed in order of priority. In other words, everything else could wait until you protected yourself. Once you secured safety, you could set up signals and such for rescue teams to find you. No matter how safe a place you managed to find, holing up there wasn't conducive to being located.

Water was a higher priority than food, but humans could last about three days without it. Forgoing drinking for so long spelled death, but as long as you left the proper signs, the rescue team would find you before then.

Considering those tenets, how was I to approach my strange predicament?

P. First of all, staying in this waterway was dangerous. The ceiling and walls had already begun to cave in, and the earthquakes—or dungeonstorms, was it? If the shaking continued and things collapsed, we could die. Getting out of the passage was best. However, one thing making the situation more difficult was Mizuho's presence. If it were just me, it would be fine. I'd survived in far harsher locales before. But I'd typically been alone. If anyone was with me, it would be comrades from the Regiment. This was different. Mizuho wasn't a soldier—she was a civilian woman.

R. Prospects for rescue were not good. I didn't know how many casualties that restroom collapse in the airport had caused, but with a big hole having opened up in the floor, they'd have to search for anyone who got caught up in it. However… If I took Mizuho's words at face value, I wasn't on Earth anymore. I would have loved to laugh that one off, but I'd already experienced things that defied reason. If I was to assume none of it had *actually* happened, then either I was on the verge of death, with my brain showing me a very odd series of images; or someone was using hallucinogens or an actress to engage in some sort of indecipherable psychological strategy against me. Perhaps British Airways's service was so bad that I'd passed out on the flight and fled into a nightmare. What made the PRWF rules so good was that even if one of those explanations were true, I'd still be doing the same thing.

In any case, I had to conclude that no help was coming. My best hope for assistance was Mizuho. I could only guess at whether her strangely named homeland, the Support Roman Empire Post Five, conducted search and rescue operations, but simply getting closer to human settlements raised the possibility of being found.

W. We had flowing water right under us, at least. We couldn't drink a drop of it without boiling it first, but if we could light a fire and find a container, that would resolve the problem.

F. This, too, I'd leave for later. We could survive for three weeks without food, and it was better for our stomachs to be growling than to carelessly eat any strange poisonous bugs or mushrooms.

My on-hand gear was less than unreliable. The rucksack only had a few possessions in it, and I'd lost it during the restroom collapse. My smartphone was gone, too. That one really hurt—even if it had fallen into the water and been rendered unusable, I probably still could have taken it apart and used the pieces for something. Losing that lithium-ion battery stung.

My wristwatch was intact. The G-SHOCK's hands pointed to three PM. It felt unreal—it hadn't even been an hour since I'd been sitting in the airport's food court eating my *tsukimi* tempura soba.

The one bit of fortune in all this was that I'd been clutching my flashlight during the quake. In this dark environment, the illumination coming from the SureFire was reassuring.

Mizuho called this place "Million Dungeon" and implied we were in a single, massive structure. The worn-down stone passage reminded me of ruins I'd seen in North Africa and Cambodia. In any case, I wanted to get out of this building soon and assess my surroundings.

As we moved, I noticed the distance between my footsteps and those behind me had widened. I turned around to find Mizuho lagging behind. She was looking down, rubbing her arms as she walked, so I stopped and waited.

"How are you doing?"

"The...the wind, it's...colder than before."

Mizuho was right. The air blowing past us was steadily growing harsher. For one with such a delicate frame, it had to be awful.

"Mizuho, that means we're nearing an open area. Just a little farther."

"Yes... All right."

Her voice trembled. She couldn't take much more of this.

Hypothermia might not sound threatening, but it was extremely dangerous. Even the world's greatest soldiers would fall dead if their body temperature dropped too low. A person's core temperature needed to be maintained in a very tight window of around thirty-seven degrees Celsius. A drop of two degrees caused hypothermia.

Plus, water drained body heat fifty times faster than air. That meant the key to avoiding hypothermia was not getting wet, but we'd long since blundered on that front.

I removed my jacket, wrung it out as much as possible, and handed it to Mizuho.

"Put this over you. Heat generally escapes through your neck and head. It's wet, so don't let it touch your skin directly—wear it loosely, like a hood."

I planned to carry Mizuho if she eventually became incapacitated, but I wanted her to walk on her own for now. The exercise would generate body heat, so it was better she moved while she still could.

After waiting for Mizuho to don the makeshift cloak, I said, "Walk a little closer to me. I can shield you from the wind." I hesitated for a moment, then said, "If you want, I can hold your hand, but—"

"Yes, please…"

Mizuho's fingers were cold as ice.

"All right. Let's slow down a bit. Focus on where you're stepping. That way, you won't trip and break your glasses."

Leading Mizuho by the hand, I resumed our journey down the tunnel. Compared with my thick, rugged fingers, Mizuho's were slight. I didn't know how old she was, but from her appearance, she could have been young enough to be my daughter.

I sighed to myself. Leading a girl by the hand as we walked—if I'd been twenty years younger, I'd have been so excited that keeping a straight gait would've been difficult. Age certainly took its toll. As a teenager, the only thing on my mind would've been how to hit on her, but now all I could think about was how to keep her safe.

"Mizuho, tell me about yourself."

I spoke to her as we walked to try and keep her awareness sharp.

"Your country… What did you call it?"

"Support Roman Empire Post Five…"

"That empire—what kind of place is it?"

"What kind of…? Well, it was made about four years ago, but I suppose it's peaceful enough."

"Four years ago? That's a pretty bombastic name for a new nation."

"History says that there was once a large country called The United States of Rome, but a military force of elves, angry over public bathwater being dumped on their lands, attacked and broke the nation apart. It's said to be why there are so many countries with *Rome* in their name in Million Dungeon. I doubt our land has any relation to the big Rome, but the name is frequently used when founding a country because it's considered auspicious."

Mizuho had suddenly gotten more talkative. As I'd guessed, she was the type who liked to explain things. The best thing to do to cheer this kind of person up was to let them speak.

"Seems like a different place than the Rome I know of."

"You also know of a Rome, Taiga?"

"Well, a little. Certainly never heard of any elves attacking it, at least."

The only things I knew about Rome came from watching the History Channel in my spare time. If I recalled right, it had been beset upon by Germanic peoples, or the Ottoman Empire, or something.

"You mean there's a Rome on Earth as well?!"

"There was, yeah."

"Wow...," muttered Mizuho. Her mind still seemed quite aware. That was good.

"If it's called an empire, does it have an emperor?"

"Yes. His Majesty the King is named Flagstand I the Deathless. The nation is presided over by his house, as well as those of the other Land-makers: a Minister, a Knight, a Priest, and an Attendant."

"What are Landmakers?"

"That's what we call those who create countries."

I see—the nation's founders are automatically the highest authorities? I thought. *I can't imagine that going well.*

"What do you do in your homeland, Mizuho?"

"I'm a storyteller. Ever since my great-great-great-great-great-great-great-great-great-grandmother's generation, we've been telling tales and singing songs."

"Then your ancestors have all lived in Rome... Wait. Didn't you say your nation was built four years ago?"

"Storytellers are the traveling sort. I've been able to settle in for now, but I've actually tagged along with caravans and adventurers all over to see more of the world. I even went to Perpetium once!"

"Wow, that's amazing."

I had no idea what that Perp-thing was; I was just trying to keep the conversation going.

"I know several stories about old Visitors from bygone days. Some are ones that my ancestors heard directly from Visitors from other worlds, and others are stories and songs about how liked the Visitors were in their former worlds. I'm really fond of them…" Mizuho sighed, sounding spellbound. "We've been shut inside Million Dungeon all our lives. It seemed like a miracle when I heard there were worlds other than this one. If there was anywhere outside this labyrinth, somewhere that wasn't a giant maze, then someday… If I can't get there in life, maybe I'll reach it in death. It's fun to think about it that way, imagining that I might be able to go to where the stories I'm telling are set."

"…Which is why you were so excited when you met me."

"That's right. I never thought I'd meet a real Visitor in the flesh. Even though you were a little different than I'd anticipated…"

"I understand you're dissatisfied, but I don't think I'm the one you should be complaining to."

"……"

"What's wrong?"

Mizuho stopped walking, so I turned around.

"I don't know. I can't feel my feet… I can't move!" Mizuho admitted, upset.

Heat left the body from the extremities. That's why one lost feeling in their fingers and toes when it got cold. As hypothermia set in, your core temperature continued to drop. Your arms and legs would stop moving, your organs chilled, and your circulatory system, reduced to its minimum function, tried to keep the brain warm. If even that became impossible, you'd pass out and ultimately die. Mizuho's body was quickly falling prey to that process.

"All right. I'll carry you."

I squatted down, facing away from her, and put her on my back. Even her legs felt chilled to the bone as I wrapped my arms around them.

"Can you carry the light and keep it in front of us?"

"My hands are numb. I'm not sure I can…"

"I should have given it to you right at the start. It's such a strong light; it probably produces a little bit of heat."

As I placed the flashlight in her trembling hands, she widened her eyes.

"It's warm! What…what star is this?"

"Star?"

"I thought this whole time that it was a tube-shaped lantern using a

searchlight star. The light from it is just so strong, so... Oh, I see—this is an item from your world, too, isn't it, Taiga?"

"I'm glad you're having fun. Try and hold out like that for just a little longer."

Standing up, I resumed our march, with Mizuho on my back. Anyone from the army would be able to tell you that this was a soldier's job—trekking over long distances, carrying heavy baggage. Shooting cool guns and fiddling with new weapons were just bonuses.

And then they'd keep marching. They'd walk carrying burdens on their backs without stopping. And they'd wait. They'd wait for orders so long that it felt like boredom might become lethal. When instruction arrived, they'd move just a little. Otherwise, nothing would happen, and they'd go home with their burdens. Such was the structure of a soldier's life. Naturally, the SAS, the world's greatest special-forces unit, was fundamentally no different. At this rate, I thought, it would be the same thing again, even in this strange new place.

I continued talking to Mizuho to keep her alert, and eventually, the end of the passage came into sight at last. Mizuho turned the beam of my flashlight away from the breaks in the stone walls to the darkness ahead. The wind whistled through the gaps, joined by the sound of flowing water.

I checked my watch. It had been about forty minutes since we'd started our trek. Assuming we'd been going at the somewhat slow pace of 4 kilometers per hour, we would have come about 2.6 kilometers. The path thus far had been an easy downward slope. Even if the inclination was only 0.5 percent, we'd have descended 13 meters.

Certainly seemed like a big building already—but this place is gigantic, I thought as we arrived at the end of the passage. And there I stood for a short time, unmoving, staring at the shocking sight before my eyes.

7

We were halfway down a cliffside. It stretched out so far, above and below, that light didn't even reach it. I couldn't see the bottom of the cliff or the sky. Several lights dotted the stone facade, faintly illuminating the walls, showing their rough, irregular formation. I looked all around, peeling my eyes, and could see several other passages and waterways like the one we'd come through. It must have been about fifty meters to the opposite side. A handful of similar openings were there, too. Additionally, I spied many cutaways of rooms, and walls and pillars that appeared only half demolished. It was like looking at a gigantic skyscraper split in two by a huge wedge.

On my back, Mizuho gasped.

"This can't be…"

"What is it?"

"Dungeonstorms always mess things up by swapping around Million Dungeon's countless rooms, but I've never heard of such an extreme change."

She craned her head to peer above.

"Incredible… You can *see* the gaps between the strata."

It would seem the situation we were bearing witness to was out of the ordinary for this world's denizens.

"We could probably move up or down from here. What area is your nation in, Mizuho?" I asked.

Mizuho swung the flashlight here and there, then started gazing intently at the walls. The tool's strong rings of light revealed the torn-apart levels of the building. Some creature that had been hiding in the dark quickly slipped away the moment it was illuminated. I caught a glimpse of its silhouette—it looked like a mouse, except it was the size of a large dog.

"Oh!" Mizuho cried out, pointing in the direction of the beam of light. "Over there! It's the statue of His Majesty!"

I squinted. About fifteen meters diagonally upward stood a white figure against the cliffside. The man was brawny, with a big beard and bare chest, but the statue was slanted like it was about to fall any moment now.

"It's the one that stands in the center of our nation's plaza. If we can get there, we can go home."

"...Oh."

"What?"

"If it was set in a common area and now it's right up against the cliffside...wouldn't that mean the other half of the plaza is gone?"

Mizuho returned her gaze to where her kingdom should've been.

"That is...what it would mean. It was a terrible storm, and I doubted we would make it through unscathed," she said, voice hard.

"We have to see how your country is doing, and quickly," I stated. "Let's hurry."

Mizuho nodded.

I let her down for now and took back the flashlight, then inspected the walls again. We could use the stones and trees sticking out here and there to make it up to the statue. The question was whether we had the stamina.

Mizuho seemed to have recovered somewhat after riding on my back, and she could manage to walk again. Still, that would only be temporary. If I forced her into a position with bad footholds, she'd end up falling.

I was freezing, too, though not as severely as Mizuho. After getting the blood flowing in our legs again with some stretching exercises, we began our careful climb.

"I'll go first and establish a safe route. You hug the side of the wall and follow me slowly."

"O-okay."

I stepped out of the flooded passage and onto the edge of a stone floor, then moved along the wall. I spied solid bedrock in the foundation, so this area seemed to be sturdy. I reached out a hand for Mizuho and brought her over. Even with her standing next to me, the floor showed no signs of collapsing.

"Good, good. Now we climb."

Ahead of us was a set of ascending steps. The stairs were made of wood and had elaborate decorations on them, but they abruptly ended partway up. My hand could reach the ground on the level above, but Mizuho wouldn't be able to get up there herself.

I placed a foot on the stairs. The sound of wood creaking echoed along the cliffside. After making it up to the top of the half-finished steps, I poked my face into the upper floor and scanned it with my flashlight. It was the middle of a passage running parallel to the cliffside. Nothing that seemed dangerous. I looked back and gestured to Mizuho. After she nervously joined me, I lifted her to the next strata before me.

Once she was there, I put a hand on the edge of the platform and pulled myself up after her. Mizuho and I exchanged nods, and then we proceeded. A ladder led higher to a trap door in the ceiling.

Opening it brought us to a room full of rubble. Fallen stones covered the floor, and bits of mortar danced in the beam of my flashlight. The portion of the chamber that faced the cliffside was wholly gone. Gazing out, I could see the other half of this room on the opposite side of the gap, separated for life.

From here, it seemed prudent to travel up a set of horizontal stone pillars that had fallen away from the wall. After getting through the chamber's debris and back out into the open, we set foot on one of the upward-slanted stone pillars. I checked to ensure my weight wouldn't dislodge it, then pulled Mizuho up. The column was about a meter thick. Beneath it was the great pit. Slipping here meant death. It was a good thing Mizuho was so light.

"Don't look down. I'll hold on to you, so keep your eyes up and scale the pillars."

Mizuho let out a scared squeal, but she went with me, her face looking desperate. Many people would be too frightened to do anything in such a high place. She was doing well.

After reaching the third pillar, I let out an exhale. There were four more columns ahead of us. "Can you see it? Just a little more. Keep going—"

But then I cut off; no sooner had I seen the pebbles falling than the shaking started again.

"Ahh!"

As soon as Mizuho let out a yelp, I grabbed the young woman and threw her and myself against the wall on our perch.

I saw a shadow overhead, and not a moment later, a huge rectangular chunk came hurtling toward us, slamming into three of the four pillars we were about to cross. The mass flattened, spewing bricks and lumber, tumbling down through the gaps in the columns. It was like an entire portion of the room had just fallen in. Having taken the brunt of the impact, all three of those pillars snapped at their bases and plunged noisily down with the rest.

The shaking came and went quickly, but the effects had been extreme. Mizuho opened her eyes, astonished. "Taiga, the path, it's..."

"...Well, that's not good."

Our way forward had vanished. Maybe we were lucky that thing didn't hit us, but now we needed to turn around in the middle of the route. Was it better to go back and find another way? I wasn't sure either of us would hold out that long.

Just then, something new sounded from above. I looked up and saw a pale-blue light shining from beyond the statue Mizuho had pointed to earlier. The glow was drawing nearer.

"Is someone there?" a man's voice asked, directing the light at us.

Raising a hand to cover my face so I wouldn't be blinded, I shouted, "Help us! I have one of your nation's people here!"

"Who is it? State your name!" came the question from above.

Mizuho shouted back, "It's me! Mizuho the Frequent Late-Nighter!"

"It's the storyteller! She's alive!"

"She's safe?!"

A few different voices exchanged words, and several sets of little, pattering footsteps came closer to us.

"Mizuhooo!"

"Mizuho, you're alive! Thank goodness!"

"Heeey, Mizuuu!"

What looked like small children were leaning out from the edge of the cliff. Mizuho waved her hand in response.

"I'm alive! I'm so sorry for worrying you!"

The man holding the light shouted, "Can you come up from where you are?"

"No, the foothold collapsed," I answered. "We're stuck."

Confused noises drifted down. I continued, asking, "Do you have any rope up there?"

"Yeah!"

"Tie it to something and throw it to us. Does anyone there know how to handle tethers?"

Knowing the best knot to use was a professional skill. I understood enough, but ropes were actually pretty difficult to handle unless you were a sailor or mountain climber. I didn't want to stake my life on an amateur's ability, hence my inquiry.

After a stir, a guttural voice replied, "I do. Give it here—let me do it."

"Oh? All right, then."

A few moments later, a heavy cord, bundled into a circle, descended. It unraveled in the air during its approach.

"I've got it! I'm tying a lifeline to Mizuho now. When I give the signal, pull her up!"

I had Mizuho raise both arms, then tied a bowline around her stomach. A safe method—once fastened, it wouldn't loosen or tighten.

"You're doing great. Just a little more," I encouraged with a smile, looking into Mizuho's eyes. Thankfully, I must have seemed a little less stern than earlier, because she grinned back.

"All good!" I shouted.

With a few voices yelling "Heave!" in unison, Mizuho was quickly hoisted up.

Now we'd do the same thing. I had them throw another rope down and pull me up this time. As I neared the top, several people reached out for me and tugged me the final leg of the way.

As I caught my breath at the feet of the tilted statue of their nation's king, Mizuho's countrymen—Romans of a sort—looked down at me. My gaze met that of a short man with a leather hood. One end of the rope was tied to the thick wooden pillar standing beyond a gathered crowd. He must have been the one who had fastened it.

"That was nicely handled," I complimented.

The man lifted his hood, looked down at me with goggling eyes, and snickered. "Of course it was. I'm an executioner. Hanging people is my specialty."

I stood up and glanced around; several looks came back from those around me—people sizing me up, gauging my worth. We stood in the semicircle remains of a town's common area. The ceiling was around four meters high, and the plaza extended ten meters from the cliff. Wooden doors and windows dotted the stone walls; they seemed connected to passages leading to homes and other establishments.

Enclosed as we were by the ceiling and walls, I would have been inclined to call the place a hall, but Mizuho and the others seemed to prefer *plaza*.

The space looked like it had once been circular, but given that it had been bisected, only half of that area remained. If that stone statue leaning against the cliffside was the concourse's midpoint, like Mizuho said, that would mean the remaining portion had collapsed and crumbled into the void.

It was certainly not a very large plaza, and people were packed into it. Hanging lanterns cast a pale-blue light, draping folk in shadows. They must have evacuated to the square in fear of further quakes. There were men and women, young and old. However, there was a startling amount of variation in their features and body types. Far more than you'd expect from even a place that saw many immigrants of varying ethnicities. No two people even had *similar* characteristics. Several had beast-like ears and fur and moved about quickly and lightly, and there was even a scaly person with a tail.

"So who might you be?" asked a man with a good physique; he looked to be about forty. He wore a patched-up apron around his waist, and he held a lantern in his hand, which was gnarled and bulky. His was the same voice that had first called out to us.

"Only polite to give your name first," I answered.

"I'm Potesara of the Free Appetizers. I was the proprietor of the Dancing Goblin, an inn facing the square—until a little while ago, at least. It's gone, along with half the square and the nation's front gate."

"I'm sorry for your loss. I'm… You can call me Taiga. And before you ask, no, I don't have a title."

"Well, that's unusual."

"I actually just arrived here from a distant land, so I'm not very familiar with this area."

"Oh—a traveler, then?"

"Essentially, yeah. I got caught in one of the dungeonstorms earlier, then ran into Mizuho while I was trying to figure out what to do. She guided me here."

I still couldn't tell how much of my identity it was safe to reveal, so I muddled my words and glanced over at Mizuho.

She had flopped down, tired, in the middle of the kids, but she still looked up and asked, "The dungeonstorm—how bad was it? What of His Majesty? Where are the Landmakers?"

A silence fell over everyone. Mizuho's expression changed.

"...No..."

"Unfortunately, yes, Mizuho," Potesara told her bitterly. "The Court was wiped out. The dungeonstorm struck the palace and temple directly. The chevaliers went to rescue them but got caught in a storm themselves; the government offices and halls were rammed into the remains of a kraken that had floated in, and everything was completely smashed. Neither His Majesty Flagstand nor any of the people in the Court survived. Support Roman Empire Post Five has been destroyed."

"No, that's..."

Others in the remains of the plaza began to voice their feelings.

"By the Calamity King's watery feet! If the Landmakers are gone, we're done for! What are we supposed to do now?"

"I knew we should have gotten insurance from Cogwheel. Chasing off that salesman last month was a bad idea."

"I was a drifter before coming to this nation anyway. Just gotta hit the road again."

"That may be fine for you, but what about the children?! Not all of us can make the journey through the dungeon to the next country!"

"That's just how it goes, eh? In this world, the weak are the first to die."

"What did you just say?"

"Eh? You picking a fight?"

"Stop, stop! Not now!"

"Pull them apart!"

"Waaahhh... Mooommyyy..."

I glanced at Mizuho and the children around her. If the people's quarrels escalated into an all-out melee, I intended to make sure they didn't get caught up in it.

However, for better or worse, that chance never came. Because once again, a terrible quake struck, slamming everyone to the ground.

8

The commotion in the remains of the concourse erupted into a cacophony of confusion and shrieks. This shaking was worse than it had been before. The masonry of the walls scraped together loudly, and loosened stones began to protrude. There came the sounds of things breaking and collapsing. A shower of dust rained down from the ceiling.

Seeing people knocked down by the vibrations trying to stand back up, I shouted, "Stay down! Stay low until the tremors stop!"

I raised my head, meaning to ascertain the situation.

"Anyone next to a brick wall, crawl away from it—it could break apart and fall on you! Everyone else, arms over your head and wait it out!"

Normally, in the case of a severe earthquake when indoors, it was safest to get away from the bases of any thick beams and evacuate to small, shut-in areas like restrooms. But with this many people packed together, giving instructions like those would have been even more dangerous.

I stayed on my hands and knees on the floor myself, waiting for the shaking to subside.

Unfortunately, it swiftly worsened. Just as I heard the booming of the quake get close to us, a rapid succession of deafening fractures sounded from somewhere below. The noise quickly grew louder, moving closer, until finally, the ground lurched. The plaza we were in was becoming a hill; one side slanted toward the cliff.

"Grab on to something!" I bellowed, ramming my fingers into a gap between the stones in the paving. As I watched, shuddering in trepidation, the floor tilted slowly, ever so slowly, its angle getting steeper.

I met Mizuho's gaze. She stared back at me, eyes opened wide in terror through her glasses. If the ground continued to turn over like this, we'd all be tossed straight to the bottom of the abyss...

Everyone had been struck speechless by fear, and even the babies had stopped their crying. Through the tense silence, the floor's slanting slowed…

…and stopped.

Just as we were about to breathe a sigh of relief, the greatest, most earsplitting roar thus far rang out. Like a bolt of lightning, or an explosion, or drumfire—but no, this impact was incomparable to those. It was enough to make me think the world had split in two.

The entire concourse itself began to slide to the side—and down the cliff.

The silence broke as everyone screamed in unison. Like a children's sled tossed down an expert ski course, the plaza and all the structures around it started slipping down toward the dark below.

The protracted rumbling had caused the cliff itself to change in shape. The exposed cross sections of rooms and passages collapsed and disappeared into the abyss. And the fissure itself was rapidly widening. As the distance between the cliffs grew, the walls, which had been close to being vertical, angled, forming a sharp slope that widened toward the top. I was witnessing the very moment of a rupture that seemed to slice the dungeon in half.

And so we slid down the labyrinth's cross section, with its hundreds of floors stacked atop one another, riding the remnants of a devastated nation.

To say it was an incredible sight would do it a disservice.

I'd once seen a sectional diagram of the Kowloon Walled City, a high-rise slum settlement that had once existed in Hong Kong and where illegal buildings were stacked up. There were rooms everywhere you went, shops and markets lined up deep inside the buildings where the outside light didn't penetrate, temples built inside torn-down sections of wall, lifelines and air ducts piercing vertically across floors… What I was now seeing was like a scaled-up version of that. With its insane construction of stone and lumber, this dungeon went on for as far as the eye could see. To my right, to my left, and above and below. Tufts of forest seemed to have been stuffed into gaps, and massive rivers formed waterfalls from floor to floor as they went down. The figures of people and similar creatures, of beasts in their packs, of strange monsters you'd only ever encounter in nightmares—I saw them all in that cross section. Yet a moment later, they were gone. This vast maze was neither quiet nor abandoned. Countless beings dwelled within it.

Million Dungeon. Now I knew just how accurate the name of this world really was.

It was at that moment I truly understood that I had left Earth.

Until now, I hadn't quite grasped the situation. I'd listened to Mizuho's explanations without objecting but had never felt wholly convinced. Could you blame me? She'd told me I'd been whisked away from my planet to another one entirely. The crazier response would have been to believe it.

But the sight before me had both the weight and the sense of reality to crush my doubts.

I really *had* come to another world.

Our downward slide stopped with an impact, its momentum sending bodies rolling across the stone paving. The chorus of screams and breaking rock ceased. Finally, the awful quake had ended. Echoes bounced through the fissure, growing ever quieter before dying out completely.

I stood up carefully.

The impact of our halt had pushed the former Romans into a single cluster by the wall. Potesara extracted himself from the mess of people trying to untangle their limbs from one another. He looked around, turning his thick neck this way and that, and slowly and nervously, he asked, "Is it…over?"

The plaza had been severely damaged by the slide. Flagstones had come loose, the wall around the outside of it had fallen starting from the edge, and the ceiling was completely gone.

"Is everyone safe?" I called out. "Is there anyone you saw before who is missing?"

People were still recovering from the terrible shock, but they called out to one another and started helping others to their feet.

Mizuho was alive as well. She was trying to stand so she could make sure the children were safe.

I stepped up to the edge of the chamber to see what state our surroundings were in. Surprisingly, the slanted-over stone statue of the king had survived. It had several small pieces missing and a few new cracks, but the sliding fall hadn't shaken it off. It must have been firmly affixed to the plaza's foundation.

I shone my flashlight around to scan things over and immediately groaned.

"Potesara, come over here for a second," I called, waving him over.

The now inn-less master wobbled over. As far as I could tell, he seemed to be taking the lead with things, and everyone else looked to him. Getting closer to him seemed a wise decision.

"What is it?" inquired Potesara.

I pointed out where the light was shining. When he saw what I had, his face hardened like stone.

"That isn't good," he remarked.

"Nope."

What remained of the concourse, atop which we all rested, was hanging precariously over the edge of a large river flowing down the slanted slope of the fissure. The concourse was barely stable right now, but another tremor could knock it loose. The river fell off acutely, not very far up, becoming a waterfall. From there, it was a straight drop.

"Everyone needs to get out of here. Potesara, could you tell everyone?"

"Yeah, I will... Shouldn't you be the one to tell them, though?"

"I'm a stranger who just arrived today—I doubt they'd listen to me so easily."

"Do you think so? From what I've seen, you're fairly experienced. You've been trying to save everyone, haven't you?"

I gave him a shrug. Potesara's lips turned up in a thin smile.

"I think I like you, Taiga, one with no title. If I still had my inn, I'd have bought you a drink."

9

Potesara returned to the others and began explaining things to them. They'd just been quarreling, so there were some apprehensions, but thankfully, people were surprisingly willing to listen. They quickly arrived at the consensus that expeditious evacuation was best. Maybe the sting had left their tongues after nearly having died twice over.

The former Romans shuffled into lines and departed from what remained of their empire. Beneath the paved ground of the concourse was a three-meter-thick layer of bedrock, barely connected. I watched from behind as the evacuees descended from the now hill-shaped area. There were heaps of stones of all sizes piled on the riverbank, which clattered under their feet as they dropped to them.

Fortunately, no untimely quakes disturbed the operation. After everyone else was out of harm's way, I carried Mizuho, who was too drained to walk on her own, and we left the plaza behind.

After crossing the rocky scree, we reached a spot where several old pillars stood on the floor, each made of alabaster marble. Judging by the numerous black soot stains, someone had built fires here in the past. The columns were over ten meters tall. They seemed to be doing a fine job holding up the ceiling—the floor of the stratum above us—so the location looked suitable as a refuge for the time being.

Determining the state of things around us was difficult because of how pervasive the dark was throughout this place. Only my flashlight and the cold light from the lanterns a few folk carried dispelled the inky black.

Other than that, I could see some lights dotting the areas along the fissure. The flames danced and swayed, evidencing either that people had set up camp or that secondary disasters were occurring.

The sound of the river flowing echoed endlessly. Despite being so

close to a waterfall, we couldn't hear the sound of the plummeting liquid slamming into the water's surface below. That meant that the
plunge basin was far down.

Flowing water would lower the temperature. It was even chillier here
by the river than it had been up above.

It was quite a bit better for me since I was moving around, but Mizuho
was seriously shivering, still wearing her wet clothes. Many other refugees were rubbing their upper arms, also feeling the cold.

I grabbed Potesara as he was walking about with a sunken look on
his face and said, "Let's start a fire. Does anyone have any kindling?"

"I'll ask."

As Potesara walked over toward the refugees, I squatted down next
to Mizuho.

"You'll be warm soon. You'll be fine."

"O-okay."

"Is this everyone? I don't know all the faces. Are we missing
anyone?"

Mizuho took a look around at the refugees before answering. "I think
all the people up there before are here. Though I don't know about the
ones who got caught in the dungeonstorms before that…"

"Unfortunately, I doubt we can go back and search for them now.
We've fallen quite far."

"Yes…" Mizuho nodded, looking depressed. Undoubtedly, there were
many she was close to whom I didn't know. I couldn't find the right
words to say to her.

Still, our own survival took priority over mourning and burying the
dead. We'd been truly fortunate to live through the slide down, but surviving the ordeal was *all* we'd managed to do. Enduring what came
after was going to be trying.

Wait. Come to think of it…

I turned back toward the river. The remnants of the Roman Empire
stood out in the dark; they were motionless, like an upside-down,
cracked pot. Chunks of rooms and passages were still stuck to the rim
of that half of the plaza, their silhouettes appearing quite tough and
sturdy.

"I'll be right back," I said.

"Huh? What are you going to do?" asked Mizuho.

"There might still be survivors. We only counted the ones who had come out to the concourse, but we didn't look in other places."

"I-it's too dangerous!"

"I'll come back the instant we get any more shaking," I assured her before leaving the refuge.

Scaling the wreckage, I went around opening all the doors I could find.

Every single one of them led to a small chamber. Each was about two by two meters and appeared to be dug out of the stone walls, with modest tables and chairs sitting inside. Bunks had been carved into the facades—they were low enough to bump your head on the top of—with blankets and thin, flimsy mattresses lying on top. Some rooms had several bunks stacked on top of one another. They were cramped, like someone had tried to make living spaces in closets or bathrooms. At first, I couldn't grasp what kind of places these were. Part of it was because the dungeonstorms had thrown the chambers into disarray. It took some time before I realized that these similar enclosures were actually living quarters.

I see…! In this world, these are standard houses!

In Million Dungeon, where there was no concept of anywhere *outside* the great labyrinth, real estate must have been an extremely precious commodity. That was why they ended up having to get as many people to live in these small spaces as possible—like in a submarine.

As it dawned on me, though, I groaned. This world certainly seemed a good bit harsher than I'd first thought. With submarines, you could surface and head to shore. The claustrophobic bunks, the constant closeness to colleagues—you just had to deal with it for a few dozen days. Yet here, that continued for your entire life.

Maybe for Mizuho and the others, that was just the way of things, but…

When I thought back, several other pieces clicked together. Mizuho hadn't seemed very put off by me being right next to her so long. She hadn't objected when I'd covered her with my body to protect her from the quake, nor when I'd picked her up or carried her on my back. There'd been no embarrassment or awkwardness—she didn't seem to feel anything about it particularly. Despite her fascination with Visitors, her bubble of personal space seemed pretty small.

And it wasn't just her—Potesara was the same. He'd come right up to me when speaking, into a range that was pretty friendly considering I was supposedly a stranger... Maybe that was just their traditional sense of distance. They were born and raised in tightly packed spaces, so perhaps it was simply how their lives worked.

Culture shock setting in, I started gathering up anything I found from the messy rooms that could come in handy. I spread out blankets and tossed everything from broken chairs to embroidery kits into them before tying it all together haphazardly and exiting. I gave special priority to anything that looked like it could be made into a tool, and any fabric as well. If there were no people who were late to escaping or unable to move, the next thing to do was haul out as much stuff that we could use to survive as possible.

As I hurried about my work, I found one door that was clearly unlike the rest.

It was a thick, wooden structure reinforced with rivets. It had a lid all the way on the bottom edge for putting things through.

When I tried to turn the doorknob, I found it locked.

I could do a little bit of lockpicking (they taught you everything in the Regiment—and just to be clear, it wasn't for burgling, but for infiltrations on secret missions and to escape when captured by the enemy), but I didn't have the tools here. Even if I did, it would probably take a while. I couldn't afford to idle about forever. But just as I thought to give up, I noticed a large metal key hanging from a hook attached to the wall next to it.

What's this now...?

First, I turned off the flashlight.

Then I took the key and tried putting it into the keyhole. It moved and turned easily.

There was a definite *click*, and I pushed open the door. Inside, it was pitch-black. Slowly, I stepped over the threshold.

And then someone hidden in the darkness sprang out at me.

10

The hushed presence, the odor of sweat, the breath inhaled at the moment of attack, and the sound of feet sliding to the side.

I turned on my flashlight.

The dark shadow, a moment away from delivering a kick to my crotch, suddenly growled and covered its face as it was overwhelmed by the sudden brilliance.

I grabbed its arm and stepped on its calf, then drove my opponent, now kneeling, into the wall.

"Ow, crap! What the hell are you doing?!"

The shrieking voice belonged to a woman.

"Apologies. Is this a prison?"

"What...? Why do you even have to ask? Can't you tell?!"

Beyond the heavy door was a room even smaller than the ones I'd been rummaging through. Scraps of straw were scattered about, and there was a wooden plank at the end of the floor, slightly higher than the rest. A fraying blanket was balled up on it. Given the awful stench in the air, it must have been a bed made on top of a toilet.

The woman, pinned down, craned her neck to look back at me.

"Who are you? You're not from around here."

"You could tell?"

"Pfft. Anyone could tell you're a stranger. Would you mind letting me go? I'm sorry for trying to kick you."

"I wonder if I should. You were about to bust my balls, and my heart's still pounding."

"Not so bad if you think of it as getting qualified to work as a eunuch. Barely any willing candidates, so it actually pays well."

I grinned and released my pin. The imprisoned woman stood up, rubbing her wrist, then turned to face me. She was a little shorter than

Mizuho, but she must have been notably older, judging by the canniness in her expression. She wore a tunic and pants, but her feet were bare. Surely, they must have been cold against the stone floor. Her hair was short and ash-colored, and it was frazzled in places. I'd already turned the light away, but it still seemed to be too bright for her; she squinted as she looked me up and down.

"Are you someone I know? We ever met? I don't think we have."

"This is the first we've met, as far as I remember. I'm Taiga. No particular title."

"No title? You lie. You're no one decent. But if you don't want to tell me, then fine. I'm Troach of the Complicated Past. A penny-pinching thief."

Troach peered out from the thrown-open prison door, examining the passage outside.

"What happened? We had one hell of a dungeonstorm rip through, and it was really shaking the place up. And then suddenly, it was quiet. What, did the country go down in flames or something?"

"You're quick on the uptake."

"Are you serious? And—Taiga, was it? What are you doing? Looting?"

"Something like that, yes. I came to find anyone who hadn't escaped yet."

"Meaning me?"

"Looks like it. Any other prisoners?"

"This is the only jail in the country. The only things left are the moles and rocklice in the walls."

All of a sudden, I could have sworn I felt something at my feet shake a tiny bit.

"Uh-oh…"

Troach looked at me suspiciously. "Huh? Did you just…?"

"We're getting out. Now."

"Eh? You can't tell me what to—"

"You'll die! Hurry up!"

I left the cell without waiting for her to respond, then ran back through the passage and returned to the square.

"Hey, what the hell is going on?!"

Troach hurried after me while I tossed her a big bundle of blankets I'd been piling up in the square. She caught them handily, the contents of the large package rattling.

"Huh? Wait, so you *were* looting the place!"

"Can you carry two?"

"Oh, you can leave that to me. In exchange for a cut, of course."

I tossed another wrapped heap of items to the suddenly cooperative thief, then snatched up two for myself, slung them over my shoulders, and darted out of the plaza. The ground was already visibly tilting.

Troach seemed to pick up on the oddity as well. "What? Wait, are we in trouble—?"

"Just run!" I shouted.

I slid down the edge of the square. Landing in the scree, I turned around, watching the remnants very quickly tilt into the river. The bedrock attached to this side came up like a seesaw, ascending. Troach poked her face out from over the edge.

"Jump down!" I yelled.

Troach suddenly made a face like a cat stuck in a tree.

"Are you kidding me?! Dammit! Out of the way!"

She hurled her two bundles down to me, then leaped.

There was no need to catch her. She landed cleanly in front of me, then crumpled onto the stone-laden ground and groaned a curse.

Before our eyes, what remained of the empire, which had been precariously perched on the river's edge, was washed away by so much water, rapidly sinking. Right before it sailed over the waterfall, for just a moment, the kingly statue poked above the surface, but the next instant, the thing was gone again, descending deep.

When I thought about it, it was just like the goddesses adorning the prow of a sailboat—it had stood at the front as we all slid down. The previous monarch had died in a dungeonstorm, but his statue had fulfilled his final duty to his people. *A reasonably tear-jerking story*, I thought. In a bit of irony, the last ones to attend to him were an outsider and a petty thief.

"...I was about to die!" Troach cried out as she jumped to her feet.

"I told you so."

"Lead with that next time! Well, I guess I'm okay, but still...," she muttered discontentedly, gathering the bundles. "Anyway, let's see what's inside... Hmm? What's all this?"

After undoing the knot in the blanket, Troach's voice sunk in suspicion. "Pots, blankets, broken chairs... Hey, this is all junk! You tricked me!"

"I didn't say a word about anything with monetary value being inside."

"You dirty bastard! Ugh... You didn't say that, did you...? Shit..."

As Troach hung her head, I stated, "We wouldn't be able to use currency if we had it anyway. Take a look around."

"Eh?"

She looked up, scanning her surroundings again...and found herself at a loss for words.

The enormous fissure that had split through Million Dungeon must have been a shocking spectacle not only for an outsider like me, but natives as well. With her jaw on the floor, Troach stared up, taking in the huge labyrinthine panorama unfolded overhead.

"...What happened?"

"I don't really know myself. All that can be said for certain is that your country has been destroyed."

"Um, that isn't anywhere *near* the problem here..." Troach's face betrayed more despair by the second.

"What is going on...? I've never seen anything like this before...," she whispered, hugging herself like this was more than she could bear. It was a bit surprising that a native of this world would be more afraid than someone who had come here without any warning. Perhaps it was a difference in viewpoint. This was all I knew of Million Dungeon, but Troach understood how things had been before this terrible quake.

"Are you all right?" I asked out of worry. The thief seemed to be in quite a bit of shock.

Troach blinked, seeming to snap out of it, and shook her head. "It's, errr... I don't want to look at it very much. It makes me feel sick. This is the first time I've ever been in such a big room."

"A big room?"

"You know, this really large place..."

"Place...?"

A moment later, I understood what she was saying.

So that's it...

The people in this world spent their entire lives in the labyrinth's tiny chambers. They'd never *seen* any room much bigger.

The term *agoraphobic* crossed my mind. The soldiers and I used to call ourselves that jokingly. Running through an open field with no cover while an enemy could be training a rifle on you was enough to get anyone sweating. However, the denizens of Million Dungeon weren't familiar with wide-open spaces at *all*, so it made sense they'd be anxious upon encountering one.

"It might be better not to look too far away until you get used to it. If you can carry those bundles, we can start a fire and get warm. Will you come?"

Troach responded to my offer with a profoundly suspicious gaze. "You're not trying to make me into a convenient pawn or something, are you, Taiga 'the Looter'?"

"I'd appreciate it if you didn't give me a title like that. And I won't force you. It's up to you."

"Well, you did just save my life. All right. I'll stick with you until I can get a grip on all this."

After handing Troach half of the things, I took the lead and began the journey back across the debris to the refugees.

"Where are we headed?"

"Some of the people from your nation survived."

"Wait…"

"The camp is just up ahead… What's wrong?"

I turned back; Troach had stopped moving.

"Are you serious? They're the ones who arrested me."

"What did you do?"

"I found someone who looked like they were hoarding valuables, so I snuck in while they were away. And for once in my life, they came back very soon after and discovered me. During our struggle, a whole bunch of people gathered…"

"Did you kill them?"

"Of course not! I'm not *that* evil. In fact, I was the one who got beat like a sandbag."

"Then everything's fine."

"The hell it is!"

"I'll smooth things over with them."

"You? The looter?"

"I told you, I'm no thief. If things get bad, you're free to run away."

"Don't need you to tell me that. Fine. I'll go, but I won't like it."

Under protest, Troach resumed her march. The pillars lined up in the dark lit up with the light from my flashlight.

"…Hmm?"

I frowned.

It had been over thirty minutes since I'd left Mizuho and the others. I'd expected at least one fire to be going when I got back, but the only thing I could see at the pillars' bases was the pale-blue lantern light.

I went up, and the refugees, discussing something with grave expressions, turned back to me.

"What's wrong? No fire going yet?"

Potesara, who came to greet me, gave me a shameful face. "Oh, Taiga. Well…"

Behind him, people were standing around a pile of several pieces of cloth. The apron Potesara had been wearing was among them. They must not have had anything they could use as fuel besides their clothing. Unfortunately, they hadn't been able to get them to light. By the looks of it, they'd only succeeded in leaving scorch marks on the heap. A bunch of what looked like thin match ends were scattered on the ground nearby, but those must have all burned out as well, because someone was desperately striking flint against steel. Though sparks flew each time they clashed, there was no sign of the flame jumping to the cloth.

"We can't get any fire going," Potesara admitted, appearing to be at a total loss.

11

That was a surprise.

In all honesty, I'd assumed they, being far more knowledgeable about the dungeon than me, would be hardy, skilled survivalists in their own right. And I had reason to believe as much.

I'd visited the jungles of Brunei for training before and learned many things from the Dayak people who lived there. How to navigate in dense woodlands, which snakes had dangerous venom, which plants were safe to eat, and how utterly defenseless soldiers unaccustomed to the environment were. It was there where I learned never to belittle native groups or cultures I didn't know anything about. That awareness helped me time and again in whatever nations missions took me to. It should have been the same even in another world like this.

However, these people were more "civilized" than I'd first assumed.

They'd lived in comfort, surrounded by their convenient tools and systems, but they were so used to the advancements of their world that if one were to toss them into a field (though the term *field* may have needed rethinking in this world), they would die quickly and pitifully.

It was entirely my mistake. I'd basically abandoned disaster victims from London or Tokyo in a refugee camp to sort it out for themselves. I shouldn't have left the area until confirming that someone could make a fire.

I said, "Sorry—switch with me. Troach! Would you come over and help?"

Troach, who had been watching from behind a pillar, suddenly gave a jolt and stiffened.

The people who had been watching the attempts to start a fire looked up, confused.

"Troach? You mean Troach of the Complicated Past?"

"Wait, isn't she that thief?"

"She was in the jail, last I heard. Didn't realize she was ali—"

Before the unrest could grow, I loudly proclaimed, "I don't know what your disagreements were in the past, but right now, we need as many people as we can get. As you can see, she's already helped me bring aid to you all. Would you trust me with her? I'll take responsibility—she won't ever steal from you again."

The people exchanged glances, seeming unsure.

"Would that be agreeable?" I pressed.

Potesara said, "Not like there's any laws keeping her in jail anymore. If you'll watch her, that's fine with us…but I don't know what the person she stole from would say."

"Who was the victim?"

"The storyteller. Mizuho the Frequent Late-Nighter."

I turned around to look at Troach, who was standing there awkwardly. "The home you burgled was Mizuho's?"

"She had all sorts of rare items, so… You mean she's still alive?"

"Yeah. Why not go give her an apology directly?"

"What? That would be *really* uncomfortable, but, well, I guess…"

I looked around, across the crowd, but couldn't see Mizuho anywhere. "Mizuho? Where are you?"

"She's sleeping over there. Must have been tired," Potesara replied.

"Sleeping…?"

I had a bad feeling about this. I pushed through the crowd, and among the faces of the refugees tired and clumped together at the base of a pillar, I spotted Mizuho. She was sitting there by herself, her head hung deep.

"Mizuho?" I called out, shaking her shoulders. Even then, she gave no reply. Her head sagged limply to one side. My jacket, which I'd left with her, fell to the ground. A touch revealed that her body was as cold as ice.

Shit! She was in the final stage of hypothermia.

"Hey, is she all right?" someone inquired.

I turned back to Troach and instructed, "Open up all the bundles we brought and get every kind of blanket you can find."

"Uh, right."

I laid Mizuho down, then untied my own bundles and dumped all their contents out. The metal objects made loud, shrill clanks and jingles that carried far, and the refugees turned to us, wondering what was happening.

A blanket, a thick cape, a tablecloth, and a bedsheet. Unfolded, they were nowhere near as much as I would have liked, but it was better than nothing.

Potesara came walking over, his eyes widening at all the things that Troach and I had scattered about.

"What's wrong, Taiga?"

"Mizuho is about to freeze to death. We need to warm her right now, but before that, we need to take her clothes off—she's soaking wet. Could you round up all the men and have them back off for a bit?"

"Y-yeah, no problem."

I didn't know what gender norms were like in this world, but considering how easily Potesara agreed, my guess that a girl wouldn't be comfortable being exposed to a bunch of men seemed correct. Getting something like that wrong now could've been trouble.

To Troach, I asked, "Could you take off her clothes?"

"What?! Are you sure?!"

"...Am I sure?"

"That's...not what I meant. Are you sure you want *me* to do it?"

"There's no time—hurry."

"All right. All right," Troach conceded, reaching for her own clothes and beginning to take them off.

I was baffled. "*You* don't need to strip! Just Mizuho!"

"What?! Oh—oh!"

"Get a grip. She doesn't have long to live like this."

I spread out the blanket I had on hand and laid it in a spot where others wouldn't see. After layering the bedsheet on top of it, I picked Mizuho up and put her down on it.

"After removing all her wet clothing, I need you to lie down with her. Roll up one—just one—of the other pieces of cloth to sit between you. Then put all the rest of it on top."

"Okay..."

With Mizuho's body in Troach's hands, I went around the pillar and moved to a place where I couldn't see them.

I could hear the sounds of wet clothing hitting the floor and cloth being dragged, after which, Troach eventually called out, "Taiga, I'm lying with her. What should I do now?"

"You don't need to do anything. Just stay there."

"...That's it?"

"That's it."

I checked in on the two of them; their heads were next to each other on the makeshift bed. Troach, seeming concerned, looked back at me and asked, "Hey, are you sure I don't need to strip?"

"What would that accomplish? Feel free if you get too hot, but your job is to warm Mizuho."

There were stories about stripping down to use your body heat to warm a victim on the verge of dying from hypothermia, but it was actually better not to. Pressing your bare skin against someone whose body temperature had lowered would rob you of your own heat, and then both would perish.

The best course of action was to get into the same bed as the freezing person, keep a blanket or some such between you, and lie there. The heat coming from your body would get trapped in the bedding. There wasn't any need for direct skin contact.

Dying together was a genuine possibility when it came to surviving with others. If one person could no longer move and you tried to help them, you could quickly both end up immobilized, and that would be it.

"I'm getting sleepy."

"Then get some rest. I have other things to do, so I'll leave Mizuho with you."

"Are you for real?"

"If anything happens, call me immediately. Good night."

Leaving the bed behind me, I gathered up several of the things Troach and I had strewed about. As I did, I quickly examined the refugees who had been watching from afar (all women, since the men had already been led away), searching for someone who looked trustworthy. For this, I had nothing to go on except my long years of observation and my gut.

Yes—you there.

I called out to a powerfully built woman of about thirty. "Excuse me! I'd like your help with something."

"...You mean me?"

There were several who didn't immediately look away when I met eyes with them. My decision was based on whose gazes were neither challenging nor covetous. This woman looked strong as well, giving her a sense of presence among the others.

With a dubious expression, she walked over to me. "I'm Taiga," I began. "Would you tell me your name?"

"I'm Savakan, She Who Strikes While It's Hot."

Reflexively, I glanced at her hands. Her palms had deep callouses on them, and the ends of her hair were tightly curled.

"Judging by your title, I'd say you're a smith. Am I wrong?"

"You're correct. But not only have I lost my hammer and anvil, I also couldn't even make a fire." Savakan twisted her lips in a display of self-deprecation.

"Can't help you with the first two, but we'll get a fire going in a moment. In the meantime, I wanted to ask you to do something for me."

"Why me?"

"Because you seem capable. Hear me out—Troach is over there right now warming Mizuho up. I prioritized Mizuho because she's in imminent danger, but there must be others who have weakened as well. It's cold here, and those with frailer constitutions will suffer—especially the children and elderly. Any wounded may be in a tight spot, too. I want you to recruit people and find anyone who isn't doing well."

"I can do that."

"All right, thanks."

Savakan returned to the other refugees and began asking around.

Good. That's one piece of pending legislation someone else can handle. The next thing I had to do was get that fire going.

12

I went to the cluster of idle-looking men a short distance away. "Sorry for the wait. Let's get a blaze going—does anyone still have matches?"

"No, there's no more. We used them all."

The frustrated answer came from a man with a dark complexion and square jaw. Unlike others, he wore simple armor made by pounding metal sheets into leather.

"And you are?"

"Lostobi the Death-Cheater... And here I thought it would be easy to light a simple fire. I was actually a mercenary before becoming a guard. I've taken many a trip into the dungeon. Always had firestarters with me, too. Not like they did much good..."

I nodded, then gave him a pat on the back. "Understood. Don't get yourself too down about it. Conditions are awful."

Lighting anything was a technical ability that required training. It wasn't uncommon to fail at igniting a fire in the wild, even *with* matches, burners, solid fuel, or any other civilized implements. In fact, in a crisis situation like this, where you first had to procure the tools yourself, starting one became dramatically more challenging.

Even modern explorers, Earth ones anyway, would only strike out once they knew all their gear was in order. Throw someone into a jungle with nothing, without letting them prepare, and most folk would die.

"Does anyone have other equipment we could use to light it aside from matches? I saw someone using flint and steel before."

"I've got them here. You want them?"

"I'd like to borrow them, yes."

Lostobi took a flint and striker out of a pouch and gave them to me.

Both the sharpened rock and the steel plate had wooden handles on them.

The theory behind using such tools was to bang the hard stone and the metal together. This caused tiny metallic shards to come off and ignite from friction. The sparks would touch whatever fuel you had, catching aflame.

Because of how extraordinarily tiny and quick-burning the scattering metal fragments were, you needed something very flammable, or they wouldn't ignite it. Admittedly, using such delicate objects wasn't the best option, but having them at all brightened our prospects. Otherwise, we would have had to make the tools ourselves. My head hurt just thinking about having to build a bow drill to start a fire.

I set off walking between the pillars, trying to find the most optimal place to work.

The first imperative when building a fire was to pick a suitable location. The wrong spot could ruin all your efforts later on. It was common sense to avoid moist or muddy ground, but there was more to it than that. If you didn't check the direction of the wind, smoke might drift into your sleeping area.

Fortunately, the airflow wasn't bad here. It passed through the pillars near the camp, heading toward the river. That suggested there was a location behind our refuge where air was slipping through. Investigating that could wait until later, though.

The stone floor was cold, but dry enough. The soot blackening the floor in spots was comforting. It meant others had successfully built fires here in the past.

I didn't know who they were, but I'd follow in their footsteps. I settled on a spot at the base of one of the pillars for the fire.

Placing my back to the pillar, I crouched down. As if in response, people gathered around me. The women had joined up with the rest again, so dozens surrounded me now.

All right, here we go. I rubbed my hands together and got to work.

Fire needed three elements.

The first was heat. The second, fuel—and the third, oxygen. A flame would only start to burn through a chain reaction of this triad.

It might seem backward that heat was needed to start the blaze, but it made perfect sense when you understood the process.

All that was required was enough to warm something small. The heat produced by the friction from rubbing wood together, the tiny combustion of powder, an electrical spark, sunlight focused through a lens, the exothermic reaction of a lithium-ion battery—there were all sorts of things you could use. Admittedly, the filament in my SureFire could likely have been helpful, but light was a precious resource in Million Dungeon; I didn't want to take it apart unless necessary. In my experience, the easiest thing to use was a magnesium firestarter, but I couldn't hope for something like that right now. All I had on hand was flint and steel. First, I'd make the embers by striking them together then transferring the sparks to the fuel.

The fuel used for this method of ignition was called tinder.

I took a scrap of cloth about the size of a handkerchief from the things I'd brought over before, placed it on the ground, and then piled up dried-out vegetable scraps, bird feathers, dry fur, clumps of dust, and anything else that looked like it might be suitable. All of it was obviously garbage, but given our desperation, these were truly irreplaceable treasures.

Looking to the small crowd, I asked, "Can someone lend me a knife? I lost mine on the way here."

As expected, several people had such blades with them. In a society where carrying weapons wasn't illegal, it was natural to see people walking around with edged tools. If I was going to be in this world for a long time, acquiring a proper knife for myself was a necessity.

Several people offered theirs to me. I chose a short-bladed one that looked easy to use, then cut a bedsheet scrap into even smaller portions. These, I rubbed into the ground, smearing soot until it was black. As I worked, I spoke.

"I need some of you to do something for me. In the stuff I poured out of those bundles earlier, there were a bunch of broken chair legs. And there should have been small wooden boxes and baskets, too. Could a few of you break them apart for me?"

Several quick-witted refugees nodded and swiftly left the crowd.

"It doesn't have to be perfect. If you can, split the chair legs and wooden scraps lengthwise. Also," I continued, addressing the ones who were still here, "it would be a big help if you could share with me any of the objects I'm about to list, or anything like them. Dried-out tree bark or resin, dried fruits or nuts, oil, used bandages, gunpowder, books or paper, clothing stuffing—basically, anything you think will burn."

Each of the people here reached into their pockets and pouches to search.

"What about clothes?" Potesara asked. "We have a bunch we were trying to burn before…"

"No, take your clothes back. You may get by with less clothing now, but your bodies will cool the more time passes. If you have any spare clothes, ask Savakan to give them to anyone who isn't looking well."

I hit the flint and steel together. There was a sharp noise, and sparks flew, briefly illuminating my surroundings. For that instant, these sparks had a temperature of over a thousand degrees Celsius. It only lasted a moment, though, so it wouldn't leave burns on a person's skin, nor would it easily transfer to the tinder.

I rolled up a small piece of garbage, then banged the flint stone and striker together in such a way that the sparks would fly to it.

The spectators began to speak in hushed voices as they watched my efforts.

"We usually just have a neighbor share their fire with us."

"My dad was angry with me for a *week* when I let the fire in the oven go out. This must have been why."

"And even when the fire went out, we could just have that will-o'-the-wisp the warlock was raising breathe on it."

"Really puts into perspective how rough it is losing your magic user."

The conversation caused my focus to snap. Without thinking, I looked up and asked, "Did you say *magic*?"

"Uhhh, yes. We had a warlock in our country. He was really handy to have around."

"The dungeonstorms took him, too. He was quite the tightfisted old man, but things do feel a bit lonelier without him."

The former Romans nodded gravely to one another. Hearing them talk so naturally about the existence of magic had me at a loss. *That's right… This world has to have magic.* Mizuho had said as much from the beginning. I wondered if Million Dungeon had anything like magic-based technology or magic-based infrastructure. The innkeeper, the smith, the ex-mercenary—they all seemed like they would be plenty used to handling fire, but if they'd gotten accustomed to such convenience, it made sense that nobody could start one.

Even so… Magic? That was an entirely unknown field to me. It was scary, not knowing what it was, the threat it posed, or how easy it was to wield. I'd have to make sure of those once things calmed down.

"Just to make sure, nobody else here can use magic, right? Nobody who could use a flame spell to solve this problem I've been working on this whole time?"

Everyone shook their heads.

"Of course not—if we could, we'd have done it already."

"Wouldn't have much trouble if we could only find a whiteheat star, though..."

I had no idea what that was, but it hardly mattered. As it stood, I was the best hope of getting a blaze going. I collected myself and resumed my work.

Finally, after several attempts with a scrap of cotton, a red point the size of a pinprick formed on it. It slowly expanded its crimson territory to its surroundings. I held up the tinder, then gave a puff, causing the oxygen-induced spark to grow larger and burst into a fire.

Surprised shouts of joy erupted around me.

I laid the remaining combustibles on the scorched floor—the bird feathers, vegetable scraps, and what have you—and placed the tiny, burning bit on top of it. I blew on it carefully, and the fire grew steadily larger.

Next, I inserted the soot-smeared scrap of cloth from before and blew on it some more. Seeing the edge of the cloth catch, I got up. A flame the size of an open palm had sprouted.

"Good. We'll make this bigger, little by little. If anyone has anything burnable, please bring it here."

More jubilant cries rang out, these ones louder than the last.

I understood why they were happy, but the tough part was yet to come.

Most of the people who had failed to start the fire stooped down to maintain it. Lighting something was easy with the right equipment. Sustaining it, however, required a constant supply of fuel.

The three elements of fire were heat, fuel, and oxygen. Adding fuel caused a heat-induced flame to grow. As it spread, you couldn't let the oxygen supply run out. This was the tricky bit. Fire suffocated without air circulation. Yet if the wind was too strong, it burned more quickly, exhausted its fuel, and died. Fire truly was a delicate thing.

People formed a pile of the sorts of burnables I had requested.

There was a length of rope from the executioner. Frayed and fuzzing, part of it was hanging by a single strand, so it wasn't usable as a tether anymore. I could straighten that out, starting from the end.

There was also a translucent clump of resin—the donator said it was for covering the strings of instruments, much like pine resin. It could be employed as an accelerant.

Someone handed me a hardened piece of white animal fat. I was told it had been taken from an animal called a sawboar. It was lard, essentially. I asked about it, and as expected, it was originally for eating; we could probably use it better as a nutritional supplement instead of burning it.

There was a dried plant vine that supposedly had been a bloodsucking kudzu vine in life. These people evidently used them for a number of things. The basket from before must have been woven out of this stuff.

No sooner had I spotted a slightly older man with a striking hair color approach than he suddenly pulled off his whole head of hair and handed it to me, leaving me in shock. It was actually a sort of plant. He wasn't making any display of eccentricity; his original hair color had also been green, according to him. He looked distraught, so I made sure it was really all right to burn, but his resolve seemed firm, and I received his offering gratefully.

Out of all the combustibles I'd mentioned, I was surprised there was no paper. Even just a single book would have been pretty useful as kindling in the initial phase, but it seemed that the material was pretty valuable in this world. What few I managed to obtain were deeds to land or buildings written on parchment in ink. They weren't worth anything absent a country.

On the other hand, a surprising number of people had gunpowder. Altogether, it still didn't amount to much, but when I inquired about it, I discovered that guns existed in this world! Not only that, but bombs and cannons, too, and they were commonly used in wars. Less deadly weapons also saw regular use, such as firecrackers to drive away dangerous fauna. I was glad I asked. I'd been wondering about it after learning they had matches. The possibility of getting shot was a significant, course-altering difference.

My knowledge of this world expanded in several directions just by looking at the items gathered here, and it was all fascinating. Still, it only brought me about 50 percent of the way to accomplishing the more important goal: getting fuel.

The burnable stuff used at the beginning, when trying to make the fire grow from the tinder, was called kindling. Thankfully, it seemed we'd have enough to go on. I fed a rolled-up, crumpled piece of parchment into the flame, followed by the torn-up climbing plant, the fraying rope, then the bloodsucking kudzu vine, going from small items to larger ones. I threw in the basket after taking it apart at that point, too. It was among the objects I'd recovered from the empire's remains.

With that, the flame was now roaring. I could see the faces of those watching nearby brighten. The light and warmth of fire were a symbol of civilization. As long as you could get one going, people would find a way to survive.

"I think there were pots and pans in the things I brought. Can a few of you go to the river and fill them with water? Filter out the sand and debris using a cloth. We're boiling it anyway, so you don't need to get the water perfectly pure," I said.

The refugees began moving energetically.

"Also, I'd like some stones we can put around this fire. Could you find dry ones and bring them here? The more, the better. Get enough that we'll have extra."

Then I began to prepare the primary fuel, the stuff that was larger than kindling. Unfortunately, this was the most scarce. At the moment, all we had were the chair legs I'd chopped and some wooden-plank scraps. It was nowhere near enough. If we needed more, we'd have to start burning clothes for real this time, but I didn't like the idea very much. There was a chance it wouldn't be enough, and the flame would die anyway.

To maintain the blaze as much as possible, I smeared the resin on a plank scrap and put it in. The fire roared with life in response.

Phew...

I leaned back against a pillar and exhaled.

This was the most we could do for the moment. Now we just had to maintain the flame while conserving fuel.

There was still no end to our worries—but the first step, at least, was complete.

13

Some people carried stones in from beyond our camp. I placed them in a circular ring around the campfire. They could shield it from any wind, slowing the burning and conserving combustible material.

As I assembled the enclosure, the water arrived. We didn't have any support strong enough to set the water-filled pots over the flames, so I piled up extra stones to one part of the circle to create a makeshift stove. It wouldn't be as effective with the heat coming from the side of the pot rather than underneath, but it was a far better option than risking the pot tipping and dousing our heat source. Foolish mistakes like that happened all the time in survival scenarios. With a lack of stamina and judgment, you'd lose the ability to do things you thought you normally could. Even dumb accidents caused by careless slipups could be fatal in a life-and-death situation, so it was best to eliminate as many contributing factors as you could.

I'd been able to save three pots from the wreckage of the empire. All of them were filled with water taken from the river, which I now boiled using the campfire's heat. The refugees waited with bated breath as the temperature slowly rose.

Outdoors, you could never drink water straight, no matter how clear it looked. Unpurified water carried a lot of pathogenic bacteria and harmful microbes in it. Imbibing any of it almost guaranteed illness or death. You always had to filter it, get the garbage out, and boil it before drinking.

It was fortunate, at least, that our camp was located near a river. Without a stable source of water, our situation would have been far grimmer.

"Potesara, you said you were an innkeeper, right?"

Potesara looked up from the crowd at my call. "Yeah—what about it?"

"Can I leave the pot with you? There was lard in the things you all brought. You could probably fashion a soup with it, at least."

He nodded several times, eyes glittering. "Leave it to me. Can't make much here, but as soon as I'm done, you get the first helping."

"I'm grateful for the thought, but give it to the children and sickly first," I replied.

Potesara and some others made an *Oh, right* face. "I'll do that," he agreed. "That's all right with the rest of you, yeah?"

None objected.

"Thanks. I still have things to do." Gathering some available stones, I got to my feet. "This is about when people's stamina will be running out. If you're tired, don't push it; take a rest. I'd like those who can still move to help me with something."

Six or seven young men and women raised their hands.

"Good. I want you to take these rocks and pile them up in several spots, each a short distance away from the ring around the campfire. Make it so that they're slanted toward the fire."

As I'd asked for as many rocks as could be found, we had quite a few left over. The piles went up quickly with all the help.

While those who'd volunteered worked, I left to go check in on Mizuho and Troach. The two seemed to be fast asleep, nestled next to each other in the blankets.

Savakan was sitting beside the bed and looked up as I came near. "Thanks for your help. Mizuho is looking a lot better."

"That's good to hear. Thanks—were you watching her the whole time?"

"I was worried."

"Where are her clothes?"

Savakan handed over the bundle, still wet. Then, using her fingers to keep count, she began reporting on the other wounded people I'd asked her to find.

"Of the children, one has an upset stomach, one's nose won't stop running, and several have scrapes and bruises, but no major wounds. One of the older folk has some hip pain. I sent everyone who wasn't feeling well over to the fire."

"Thanks. You should make your way there, too."

"Okay. I'll wake these two up and take them with me."

Upon my return, erected in four spots were stone piles slanted at sixty degrees about one meter away from the campfire.

"What are these for anyway?"

"Sitting against?"

The youngsters who'd erected the piles tilted their heads in confusion.

"They're for reflection. The heat from the campfire bounces off them, making it even warmer," I explained, unfolding Mizuho's clothing and hanging them on the stacked stones. "And if you do this, we can dry laundry."

That earned many impressed remarks, making me feel like I'd just become the presenter of some weekday daytime television show.

Survival life hacks taught by a former SAS member. That could probably work as a show. I could blur my head, put my voice through a voice changer... I tried to imagine that TV producer who had contacted me after my discharge and what his face would look like if he heard my idea.

As I started to mull over things I couldn't do anything about, a nice smell drifted by my nose. I looked toward the campfire. Potesara had begun dishing out metal containers filled with soup from the pot. Someone seemed to have picked up all the things I'd scattered about earlier. I remembered tossing a bunch of dinnerware and cooking utensils into the bundles; I was glad they were proving to be helpful.

"That's a pretty good smell you've got going," I called out.

Potesara grinned in satisfaction. "When I asked if anyone had anything to eat, I got more than I expected. Scraps of bacon, old herbs, stale bread. Quite a bit, all told."

The children took the first sip of their soup, then cried out that it was too hot, causing laughter to spread around the campfire.

"It's a thin soup, and there isn't much, but if I keep adding water and ingredients as I go, we should have enough for everyone."

No sooner had Potesara said as much, relief plain on his face, than I heard Mizuho shriek, "What?! Huh?! What is this?! Why?!"

She had regained consciousness, stood up, and was staring hard at Troach.

"L-look, it's not what you think!"

"What isn't what I think?! Why am I naked?!"

As Mizuho held a blanket up to her chest and tried to move away from Troach, Savakan made an attempt to calm her. "Mizuho, calm down. Troach was trying to help you—"

"Troach? Help *me*?"

Mizuho blinked her eyes.

"Y-yeah, that's right, I was trying to..."

"Really? You weren't trying to violate me because you didn't have the chance last time?"

"O-of course not! Well, sure, something like that may have happened before, but—"

"I knew it! You beast!"

"I told you, this time is different!"

I breathed a sigh of relief at the exchange. That Mizuho felt well enough for such a back-and-forth was a good sign.

I leaned back against a pillar a short distance away and sat down. Even I was a bit tired after all that. As I basked in the comforting heat coming from the campfire, I zoned out, trying to recover my stamina—when just then, a child came over to me. He was a boy who must have been four or five.

"Mister!"

"Hmm?"

"He said to give you this."

In his outstretched hands was a small metallic cup. It wasn't soup inside—it was a slightly brown liquid.

"Thank you... What is it?"

"Tea!" was all the boy said before he went back.

I brought my nose up to it and caught a fragrant whiff of roasted nuts.

"Potesara! Are you sure I can have this?" I questioned.

He answered, "You've done enough to deserve it, Taiga!"

Did I? Well, I hope so.

I brought the cup the boy gave me to my lips and took a sip of the hot beverage. It was completely different from the black tea I knew. The flavor was foreign to me, but not displeasing.

I was pretty sure Mizuho was the only one who knew I drank tea. Had she told him while I was away, or had Potesara just put it on for me as a show of appreciation? Regardless, I was grateful to have it. I took my sweet time savoring this first cup since being spirited away to this world.

14

It seemed all right to leave the fire to the others for a while, so after I drank my tea, I closed my eyes and went to sleep. Getting rest when you had the chance was the trick to being a soldier. I'd slept in much worse places before. It was dry here, without any awful stenches, and it was warm close to the campfire.

The issue was that this wasn't the Earth I knew, but a totally unknown planet…

After about an hour and a half, I opened my eyes. Not even I was able to sleep very deeply in our present predicament. I felt like I'd just had a nightmare that combined *The Lord of the Rings* and *Black Hawk Down*.

I shook my head to drive off my drowsiness. Around me, it was quiet; maybe everyone had gotten their soup. People nestled close to the flame, talking in soft voices. Many others were sleeping. The children, in particular, had been put to rest in one big clump inside a mountain of blankets.

Mizuho, bundled up in a blanket next to the campfire, was engaged in a fervent discussion with Potesara. Opposite them was Troach, who was starting to nod off. Her head looked to be in the right position to fall on Savakan's shoulder.

Walking over and sitting down at the fire ended up making me pretty uncomfortable when everyone started staring at me at once.

"Is everything all right?" I inquired.

"Oh yeah." Potesara nodded, passing a metal bowl to me. Soup was in it. "Your helping, Taiga."

"There's a lot in here…"

"It's what collected on the bottom of the pot. Nobody here's complaining."

"Well then, thank you."

I sipped at the broth. The flavors of the meat and vegetable scraps had already seeped out, but an empty stomach was the greatest spice of them all. I downed the soup within a few eyeblinks and set the bowl down.

"That was good. Thanks for putting this together for me despite the awful situation."

"We're the ones who owe you the debt of gratitude. I was surprised when I first heard, but it seems you've been through quite a bit more than we have."

"What are you referring to?"

"You came here from another world, didn't you?"

Hearing that from Potesara, I looked at Mizuho. She'd been watching me silently until now; when our eyes met, she nodded.

"I told everyone you're a Visitor."

"Not that I mind, but... Do you all really believe that?" I asked.

Potesara answered for Mizuho this time. "Well, we *have* to. You don't seem to know a thing about Million Dungeon—and I've never seen such a bright lantern before, either."

That last part was referring to my SureFire.

"Visitors are the stars of all kinds of tales, so many know of them," Mizuho explained. "Several have probably come from your Earth in the past, too. Million Dungeon continues to grow in every direction—so much so that some theorize it's connected to a great many other worlds."

"The ruin of our nation was a disaster, and our current situation is unavoidable, but we all know where we are," Potesara remarked. "But you, Taiga—you're facing down two troubles at once. Not only have you wandered into a place you know nothing about, but you've also gotten mixed up in this catastrophe. You've got it worst of all, and yet you still did your best to help us..."

"Yeah, Taiga, just who the heck are you anyway?" Troach appended, having perked up out of her nap. "No one normal, I know that much. But I've never met a man like you. It's like you can do everything on your own."

"That's not true. Nobody can do *everything* themselves. I just happen to possess training for these sorts of things. And I didn't do it all myself here, either. You did your jobs, too."

"Still, we all have you to thank for our safety," Mizuho stated. "What sort of person are you exactly? What did you do back home?"

The question left me feeling curiously embarrassed. What *had* I been up to? To be perfectly blunt, I'd fucked up, quit the Regiment, and was drifting along. Explaining as much wasn't going to help these people comprehend, though.

"I was…in the military. A soldier."

"Did you fight in wars?" pressed Mizuho.

"You could say that."

Irregular combat and secret operations could be considered as such. It was likely different from what they knew battle to be. However, just as I thought that, the guardsman Lostobi, having listened from behind Savakan, spoke up.

"Is that right? I've been a merc a long time, but I've never seen anyone like you. They were all violent and loudmouthed. Not one of them would help anyone if there was no coin in it for them."

"The unit I was in… Well, it was a bit *special*. Our creed was to carry out our work as quietly and inconspicuously as possible."

Lostobi widened his eyes. "Were you an assassin?"

"That depends on how you define *assassinate*," I responded, deflecting. Lostobi nodded several times, seeming to have convinced himself.

Potesara rubbed his jaw and said, "I get it. A soldier, eh? A pretty good one, from the looks of it."

"I'd hope so."

"No, you're definitely one hell of a fighter. There aren't many out there who would jump in and rescue people they don't even know."

I shrugged, not answering. My comrades in the Regiment probably all would have done the same. Well, maybe not *all* of them. A few who'd hesitate came to mind.

"On that note, Taiga the Visitor—we have a special favor to ask of you," Potesara said, straightening up. The others eyed me with serious expressions as well.

"What is it?"

"We think you should be the King," the man stated.

"King…?"

I looked to Mizuho. She nodded emphatically. "Our nation has fallen, torn apart by the dungeonstorm. We've been cast into the dark labyrinth with naught but the shirts on our backs. I can say one thing for certain: Without you, we all would have starved to death, died of thirst, or been eaten by monsters."

Troach took over from there; her look a more docile one. "If you hadn't arrived, I'd have bit it, too. I may be a moneygrubbing burglar, but I don't let my debts go unpaid."

"We all watched you run around and put us all to work," Savakan chimed in. "So while you were sleeping, we had a talk. Everyone's in agreement."

The next thing I knew, all the refugees around the campfire were staring. Mizuho, Troach, Potesara, Savakan, Lostobi, the executioner, the green-vine man... Every person still awake, without exception, had their eyes on me.

"We'd like you to be the King of our new nation, Taiga the Visitor," Mizuho repeated.

15

"…Hold on. Would you quit joking around?" was the first thing out of my mouth. "A king? Me?"

"Yes. We want you to be the leader of our kingdom."

Mizuho's face was dead serious as she answered, which only served to make me even more confused.

"Look. If you trust someone who just *happened* to be able to start a fire with an entire *nation*, you're going to have a bad time."

"We're already having a pretty bad time," Troach objected irresponsibly. "It can't get any worse than this."

I glared at her. "You could starve, you could get sick, you could die… It could be *much* worse than this."

"But you'll do your best to make sure that won't happen, right?" she countered. "You worked so hard for people you'd never seen before in your life. There's no point being humble about it now."

Voices expressing their agreement sounded from all around.

Understanding that this was not a farce, I finally started to panic.

Being in charge of people was something you were either meant for or not. Ineptitude spelled disaster in such a field. Simply put, I wasn't cut out to be a politician. Most of all because I had no desire for authority. In a leadership position, this was not necessarily a virtue. It would only serve to confuse those under me.

"Wait. Just hang on a second. Any decent person would try and help if they saw civilians in a crisis. That has nothing to do with whether you can have them manage a *country*."

"But when you were leading us, giving us instructions and orders, you did wonderfully," Potesara asserted. "You can't do something like that without experience managing people."

"I only could because there are so few of you. The most I've ever led was a platoon."

"And how many people are in a platoon?"

"Depends on the situation, but no more than fifty or sixty."

When I answered Mizuho's question, the others began to mutter among themselves.

Clearly, they had misunderstood, assuming I'd been some sort of general.

But that's all cleared up now. Good thing, I thought just before Troach said something that made me doubt my hearing.

"Oh, well, that's more than enough."

"...What?"

People exchanged looks, nodding, convinced.

"Fifty or sixty is quite a bit more than we need."

"Yep, that's right. It's perfect!"

Mizuho and Troach nodded to each other, seeming to have come to a consensus. When did they get to be such good friends? I had a bad feeling about this. As I frowned, Mizuho continued:

"We have thirty people here now. That might not be much, but... Others will start flocking to us once they hear we've created a nation."

That's when it hit me. I was the one laboring under the wrong impression.

"Just so I know, when you say 'nation,' how big of a population are you usually talking about?" I asked.

Mizuho answered immediately. "There are four we call the *world powers*, and they have thousands, if not tens of thousands of people. The rest are more varied, but most of them are what we call *tabletop kingdoms*, and the majority only have around thirty people."

I was dumbfounded.

The "countries" in Million Dungeon were incredibly tiny. Now that I thought about it, this world was sectioned off into all those labyrinthine strata. Forming civilizations like those on Earth was impossible. It seemed likely that Million Dungeon didn't have a large population to begin with.

"...What about your nation?"

"You mean Support Roman Empire Post Five?"

"Yes, that."

"It had over a hundred people! I hear there were only fifty when it was founded."

"...I see."

I rubbed my hands into my face as I thought. It would have been better had I kept quiet. Unknowingly, I had walked right into this.

"Please?" Troach said. "Say you'll do it. It's not like we'll be making you do *all* the boring stuff. I'll be in your Court, if you want."

"That's right—me too!" Mizuho added.

"What does that mean?"

"Just what it sounds like!" Troach replied. "It means we're gonna be Landmakers now!"

Landmakers...?

My face must have betrayed my confusion, because Mizuho and the others launched into a multipronged explanation assault.

According to them, this was how it all worked...

Million Dungeon had not always been an expansive labyrinth of caves and tunnels. Initially, it was a "totally normal" world, one with sprawling lands where humans and other species could thrive.

But at some point, a great disaster called the Dungeon Calamity occurred. The labyrinth began to form on its own, rapidly proliferating until it covered the entire world. It swallowed land, sea, and sky, separating people from one another with layers of stone and piling up many more strata.

It destroyed the world as they knew it, and everyone was left to rot away inside the dungeon.

"However, not all succumbed to despair. Some stood up to create kingdoms in the darkness. They brandished the light of stars to shepherd the wandering people, coming to be called Landmakers."

As though she'd given this sort of introduction many times before, Mizuho spoke with a flowing smoothness, adding in hand gestures for emphasis.

"They challenged the dark, slew the monsters that preyed on humankind, and established new domains for the dungeon-dwellers—and in so doing became a symbol of hope for the hopeless."

She suddenly pointed her fingertip at me.

"If you would become our King, Taiga, I will gladly make my decision. I shall undertake the nation's internal affairs as Minister of your Court."

"Yeah, me too," Troach piped in. "I'm actually pretty quick-witted and good with tools. You can use me as the Attendant."

With the pair looking at me, I threw the conversation over to Potesara and Savakan. "What about you two?"

They regarded me with surprise and shook their heads.

"Ha! I'd never take such an important position. I'm just a regular old innkeeper."

"And I'm only a smith. I'm good at making swords, but I can't swing them for beans."

Their replies had me confused. They acted like I'd just asked something utterly inconceivable. In the meantime, Potesara said, "Landmakers are *special*, you see? We normal folk don't even consider striking out into the dark of the dungeon. You'd have to be a foolhardy sort, like a band of mercenaries or merchants, an adventurer or a salesman… Otherwise, the only thing on your mind would be to get to the nearest nation and try to live in relative safety."

Savakan continued, "And even the foolhardy ones seldom decide to take charge of others and make a nation. That's why Landmakers are so special, and why everyone wants to follow them."

I returned my gaze to Mizuho. Compared with the well-built Potesara and Savakan, she was much shorter and more slender.

"Are you one of those, er, foolhardy types, too, Mizuho?"

"Taiga, that child was born into a family of storytellers. Her clan has always traveled the labyrinth, moving with armed caravans and such. You'd do well not to underestimate her."

I gave a surprised look. Mizuho narrowed her eyes a little as a subtly confident grin spread on her face.

"Does that go for Troach, too? She's, well…"

It seemed a little beyond the norm to have someone imprisoned for theft as part of a court. Still, I hesitated to say as much in front of her.

Realizing what my stammering signified, Mizuho said, "The act of stepping forward to be a Landmaker holds an important meaning in and of itself. The words alone are enough that dozens of people will be willing to follow you."

"Yeah, that's right! I've been working alone this whole time. Despite what you may think, I've gotten through some pretty rough situations myself."

"Indeed. I haven't forgotten how you snuck into my room *or* what you tried to do to me, of course, but that is a separate issue."

"I told you, that was a misunderstanding! Well, part of it anyway. But still…"

Ignoring Troach's excuses, Mizuho continued, "This actually isn't a bad deal for you, either, Taiga. You know next to nothing about this world, don't you? If you become our King, I can teach you."

"Thanks, but…"

"Then it's settled! And excuse me for saying it, but it's not like you have anything left to lose."

I had to laugh at the remark.

It reminded me of Colonel Kurtz from *Apocalypse Now*. Deep in the jungles of Vietnam, he was a soldier who acted like a king, leading the locals and essentially constructing his own nation… Wouldn't I turn out the same as him if I were to accept this responsibility?

I didn't like it. Coming all the way to another planet just to play as the ruler of a castle? What clumsy writing that was.

Still…

…what would happen if I refused? They might install a different leader. It might be Mizuho, or it could end up being Potesara or Savakan. Would I be able to leave them alone? No. Soldiers in the Regiment were built to face crises. I could never even think of abandoning them. In other words, my acceptance or refusal really didn't make much difference—the title of "King" aside, that is.

"…All right, fine."

I looked up.

"On one condition. I believe, to begin with, that the King should be chosen from one of you. Until a suitable person is found, I'll accept the position of Landmaker."

Troach cocked her head. "I don't get it. You mean you don't want us to call you the King?"

"Yeah."

This is probably gonna annoy them, I thought.

Yet, upon hearing that, Mizuho answered smoothly, "Then you should be the Ninja."

"Yeah, the Ninja. That would work."

The words coming out of Mizuho's and Troach's mouths caught me completely off guard.

"Ninja? Did you just say *ninja?*"

"Yes."

"Yep!"

"By 'ninja,' you mean the people who dress in all black and have katana...?"

"Yes, and throw *shuriken.*"

"And use ninjutsu!"

"They're the Court member in charge of information gathering. Don't you think that would be perfect for you?"

"Yep, fits like a glove. How about it, Taiga?"

"Uh... Sure."

I nodded and agreed...but something still felt odd.

Mizuho pounded her hand with a fist and stood up. "Then it's decided! Taiga, currently title-less, will be our Ninja and acting King. I, Mizuho the Frequent Late-Nighter, will be Minister. And the Attendant will be Troach of the Complicated Past—the three of us will form the Court. Let's create our new nation right here!"

A cheer sounded, echoing off the forest of pillars in the camp and traveling into the endless expanse of Million Dungeon.

Talk of a coronation ceremony and a celebratory feast began, but we had no alcohol or food. Postponing the event was the only option, though everyone's mood still visibly brightened.

Mizuho took the initiative on holding a meeting on something she insisted was essential: a name for our nation. The one chosen was the Great Camp Bravo Kingdom. Obviously, the moniker was utterly nonsensical. It made me fear for the fledgling country's future.

Once the discussions had settled, everyone decided to get some rest, since it was already very late. It had been dark in Million Dungeon since my arrival, so I figured that was just how it was, but apparently, there was a day-night delineation here.

Everyone nestled into their own sleeping spots. I caught Mizuho before she lay down, however.

"I wanted to ask something... You said there are a few stories of Visitors who came here from Earth, right?"

"Yes, I did. Why?"

"How about any where they made it back to their original world?"

"Well..." Mizuho trailed off. When I waited for an answer, she continued uncomfortably, "...There *are*, but very, very few. Most tales of

Visitors end in tragedy, with them losing their lives in Million Dungeon. Any others are triumphant recountings of their deeds and accomplishments."

"I see."

That figured... As I suspected, returning to Earth wasn't very probable.

"Oh, but wait! Um, it doesn't seem all that common, but...," Mizuho said, seeming to have recalled something. "There are a few stories where the Visitor ends up finding a home in Million Dungeon and living here happily... And, well, that is..."

"I see. Thank you," I replied, smiling a little.

She was probably trying to comfort me. Even so, she'd still mentioned how rare any kind of success for a Visitor in Million Dungeon was. That sort of honesty seemed very like her.

16

I slept for about five hours before waking up. Right away, I looked toward the campfire. Several people were already up and around it, speaking in hushed tones. I went over to see. Weakening the flame by putting some ash on it before sleeping had proven effective—the campfire was still burning slightly in the embers, without actually producing much of a visible flame. Blowing on it helped strengthen it, and I added some wood.

We had almost no fuel left on hand.

The refugees were steadily waking up, too. After asking someone else to tend to the flames, I left.

I departed the camp and descended to the rubble heaps. It was brighter here than it had been the previous day. I looked up and saw several bright spots in the now-exposed labyrinth cross section. Most of them were in the same places as the light I remembered seeing last night, but they'd grown brighter.

Mizuho called this sublime canyon that had split apart Million Dungeon the Great Fracture. She claimed that no disaster like this had ever happened in all their history, but I was a bit skeptical. Not only were paper and stone tablets their only means of recording information, but everyone was divided by the labyrinth. Even if something *had* been documented, getting it to some sort of large, shared repository couldn't be easy. That was why storytellers like Mizuho traveled around, imparting knowledge through word of mouth. Either way, none of this world's denizens had ever witnessed such a cataclysmic upheaval before. This sort of thing hadn't occurred even during the Island Whale's Sleep-Tossing or the Dungeon Tsunami in the distant past.

I heard footfalls behind me. Mizuho had caught up.

"Morning."

"Good morning…," she replied with a yawn.

Pointing to the wall of the Great Fracture, I asked, "Any idea what those lights are?"

"Lights… Oh, those? Those are stars."

"Stars…?" I repeated, tilting my head.

Mizuho snapped her eyes open. "Oh! Now I remember—in your world, stars sit in the 'sky.' They don't come down, right?"

"Right…"

"A lot about this world is pretty different. The Dungeon Calamity didn't take much time to swallow everything up, so even the stars said to have hung in the 'night sky' couldn't escape. Those are the lights of star fragments, buried within the labyrinth."

"They're brighter than yesterday," I remarked.

"Well, of course… Daytime is brighter than night, after all."

Judging by Mizuho's face, I'd made another odd comment.

"Which means when they're bright, it's daytime, and when they're dark, it's night?"

"That's correct!"

According to her, stars came in many varieties. These included calendar stars, which waxed and waned at regular intervals, and firefly stars, which could be used as portable sources of illumination. (She mentioned these were the objects within lanterns, which was something I'd been curious about for a while.) Not all the stars were cold, either; some gave off warmth, like whiteheat stars, which were hot enough to boil water, or infrared stars, which people used as body warmers. There was a myriad of types, all employed for different purposes.

"They sure aren't anything like the stars I know," I commented as I listened. Mizuho actually opened her lantern and showed me a firefly star. To me, it appeared like a naturally luminescent crystal.

"What are your stars like, Taiga?"

"They're very far away in the sky, and incredibly big. Each one moves in a path over exceptionally long periods of time."

"We apparently have ones like that, too. I've never seen any, though. I hear they're massive and take forever to make a complete course through the labyrinth. Apparently, you can tell exactly where they go from the beautiful circular passages they leave behind."

Among the little visible stars, shadows were moving here and there.

It was hard to make out since the glowing things were distant and the light was scant, but I could see what appeared to be groups gathered at a few spots.

"There's people over there, right? What are they doing?"

"Where?"

"The right part of the wall—third star from the bottom."

Mizuho peered as hard as she could through her glasses but eventually shook her head in resignation. "I can't see it at all. You must have good eyes to see that far."

"Not really...," I started before it hit me.

Given that she wore glasses, Mizuho must have had poor eyesight, but maybe everyone who lived in Million Dungeon had weaker vision in general. If they lived their whole lives in a dungeon, they wouldn't need to see very far.

Which meant it was natural to assume that many of these people could probably see better in the dark at limited distances. Making assumptions based on what I knew from Earth would be dangerous.

Mizuho took her glasses off and rubbed her eyes before putting them back on.

"I can't see them, but they must be people who live nearby gathering to harvest the star. They could also be crossing-fish or burrowing-birds—they like to flock around stars, too."

"If they're people, should we try calling out to them for help?"

"I wouldn't. We could be attacked."

"Should I assume others are hostile, then?"

"They're not necessarily *all* dangerous, but adjacent kingdoms always end up in territorial disputes. And many races view humans as enemies."

"Like the elves you mentioned yesterday?"

"Not only them. Humans are among the weaker inhabitants of Million Dungeon."

Under the (relatively) bright morning light, mist coming off the river licked at our feet. The wind blew from the bottom of the Great Fracture, causing the morning fog to shiver and squirm like a living creature before disappearing into the air.

A few people who had left the camp were standing around, beholding the incredible sight. It was just as much an unbelievable sight for them as it was for me. Yet still, their faces shone with the drive to create a new kingdom, despite having lost their old homes and neighbors only the previous day.

Potesara was among them. The ex-innkeeper had taken a seat on the outskirts of our little haven, and tears were dripping down his cheeks. Mizuho quietly told me his wife and son had been carried away with the inn.

The people they'd been separated from hadn't necessarily died in the dungeonstorm, but in a complex this vast and confusing, who knew what the chances of finding them were?

"Mizuho, what about you…?" I asked.

She shook her head and smiled a little. "I was living alone…but I'll never see more than half of the people who always came to listen to my stories again, and thinking about it makes me feel lonely. I'll have to make sure I don't forget any of their names."

That was all she said.

So that's how it is, I thought. This world's inhabitants were strong. Constantly exposed to a hostile environment, they were well aware of their own weakness. Their safe and peaceful lives of today could be gone the next day. Accepting that and getting on with their lives was the only recourse. The people of Million Dungeon were a lot like locals living in an area of constant warfare.

Feeling as though I understood their mindsets now, I felt respect for them. However, I also knew that it wasn't my place as an outsider to say as much without forethought.

Thus, I said nothing as the refugees shed their tears in the morning mist.

17

"Let's get right to it. I want to talk about what we should do now."

After finishing breakfast (hot water with a tiny bit of flavor to it), we began our first meeting.

The conferences held by Landmakers to discuss their nation's future were apparently called Round Tables. Unfortunately, we, the Great Camp Bravo Kingdom, hadn't a single table. Instead, we gathered around the campfire, which was still barely going even after conserving our fuel. Behind Mizuho, Troach, and I were the other twenty-seven citizens, pressed together to listen. The Court would have no secrets.

"The most dangerous issue we have currently is—," I began before noticing that Mizuho seemed to have something she wanted to say. I'd almost forgotten. I was better off leaving this to her—she *was* the Minister.

"Mizuho, if you would?"

"Gladly!" Mizuho stood up, cheerful. "Thank you all for gathering here today. I am Mizuho the Frequent Late-Nighter, and I'll be acting as chairwoman."

"Wooow."

Shooting a glare over at Troach, who was fervently applauding, Mizuho continued. "No applause is necessary. Our kingdom's only campfire is located right here, and the firewood we use as its fuel is about to run out. Unless we secure more by the end of the day, we will be in an extremely rough situation tonight. We need burnables— and fast."

Some people voiced their agreement.

"Our second issue is food. We need to secure food for thirty people. Humans can only live without food for— How many days was it, Taiga?"

"Technically, about three weeks—but only if we're in a situation where there's hope of rescue. We can't afford to spend that much time."

"Indeed. I think we'd all rather pass on going into the dungeon on an empty stomach and being stuck there."

"Fuel and food…," Troach stated, her face grave. "So basically, we'll have to bring in plenty of wood and meat, right?"

Mizuho gave the other woman a look of disapproval. "There is no 'basically' about it. That's *exactly* what we'll do."

"Then say as much sooner next time."

It seemed like the two would get into a fight if left to their own devices, so I raised a hand to draw their attention. "I don't have much knowledge here, so please tell me how we can obtain wood and meat in the dungeon. In my world, trees didn't grow without light from the sun."

"What is 'the-sun'?" Troach inquired.

I recoiled. *Right, right…* "The sun is an extremely bright star… It shines in the day, and it's hidden at night."

"Oh? That's the same as it is here. In the dungeon, trees grow in places where there's bright stars, too. We'll have to find one of them."

"I see. What about meat?"

This time, Mizuho replied. "We have several options for that. There are beasts in the labyrinth, as well as mushrooms. We haven't tested it yet, but we might also be able to fish in the river. We could use anything edible."

That reassured me a little. The environment was alien, but these people didn't differ all that much from me. The things we needed to do to get by were similar.

"All right. No time to waste, so let's hurry."

"Hold up," Troach interjected as I went to stand up. "Don't get ahead of yourself. We have to decide how many people we'll bring."

"What do you mean?"

"We're about to enter the labyrinth, right? It can't be just the three of us."

I blinked. "I don't understand."

"Come on now, Taiga. We want to bring as much lumber back as we can, and game to fill everyone's bellies, right? Who's gonna carry all that?"

"…Right."

She was correct. We didn't have any transport planes or trucks, so we'd have to carry or drag everything we harvested back to camp.

"...Errr, sorry, Troach. I assumed you, the Attendant, would carry back thirty people's worth of stuff."

Laughs went up at the joke.

That wasn't good. I couldn't get a handle on this world's common sense, and now even natural laws were suspect. And here I'd just thought that our common humanity would mean all the basics were the same.

As the laughter died down, Mizuho got back on topic. "If there are no objections, I'll choose the people to go with us. Taiga and Troach probably can't make quick judgments as to character."

"Probably not. Anyway, I'm just the Attendant. I don't have to manage anyone else."

"All right. We'll leave it to you."

I pondered for a moment on who to bring along as a subordinate but stopped myself. I was the one who knew the least about what awaited us in the labyrinth. Me leading anyone else was out of the question.

We were going into the dangers of the dungeon, and we'd have to bring along regular people rather than going ourselves.

As I watched Mizuho talk to the citizens and pick out our team, a feeling of unease began to well up within me.

This seemed insane. Shouldn't the three of us go alone? Or better yet, just me? Weren't there horrible monsters and dangerous traps waiting for us in the dungeon? Tossing a bunch of regular people into that situation seemed a poor choice.

True, the three of us in the Court wouldn't be enough, but still...

Mizuho, oblivious to my deepening anxieties, seemed to have finished her selection. "Taiga, I've chosen nine people in total. All of them have ventured into the dungeon as subordinates before. It isn't many, but any more would be overdoing it..."

"So we're taking a third of the citizens with us? Seems like quite a bit already."

"Don't you think it's appropriate considering that you, Troach, and I will be taking charge of them?"

"Wait—I don't need subordinates. And we could probably get by with just six laborers."

"But the King himself not having a single subordinate would be—"

"I'm not the King. I'm a representative."

"Ninjas need help, too, don't they?"

"They do not!"

We argued a bit, but I firmly refused to get an assistant for myself. In the end, we settled on six others. That was still too many for me, but it was the lowest number Mizuho and Troach agreed to. In hostage-recovery missions, my group and I would be the only ones entering enemy territory, so all we had to think about was getting the captives out. This flew in the face of that; we'd be leading six *into* enemy territory and still had to return with everyone safe.

"Next up is me, then. We good?"

Troach picked up a piece of charcoal and drew a square on a stone pillar in a position where everyone could see.

"This is where we are now. Our camp. No, the *palace*."

I looked up with surprise. By her declaration, from this very moment, this cold, bleak plaza filled with stone pillars was no longer a refuge where the people of a lost kingdom would band together, but the center of a new nation.

It seemed I wasn't the only one who felt it. Everyone's expressions shifted, and I could physically sense the mood sharpen.

Troach, perhaps realizing the weight of the words she'd spoken, chuckled as though recoiling from them. "Well, we still don't have a single throne, though. Anyway, the only thing we have in our kingdom right now is this one room—a palace, but only in name. And…"

Troach drew a straight horizontal line below the square.

"…here's the Great Fracture. This direction would be south."

It wasn't until later on that I asked, but Million Dungeon had compass directions just like Earth. They used six cardinal points: east, west, south, north, up, and down. Pathfinding was conducted by way of northpole stars, which always pointed north. (This wasn't the North Star as I knew it from Earth, but rather a tiny star fragment in the shape of an arrow that you could walk around with.)

After adding an X on either side of the square, as well as two short lines on the outside of it, Troach turned back to look at us.

"To the east of the palace is a mountain of rubble. West is a thick wall, and at a glance, we won't be able to get past either of these. There's an actual passage leading north. Meaning our best shortcut would be to blaze a trail in that direction."

Mizuho widened her eyes. "I'm surprised. When did you have time to scout all that out?"

"I took a peek around sunup... Look, I'm a high-and-mighty Land-maker now, too, right?" Troach said, seeming embarrassed and looking away. "A-anyway! It's easy. We just go into the northern passage, find what we need, and get out. That's it. Right?"

After a breath, I nodded. "Yeah—should be simple."

It looked like Mizuho and Troach had each done what they'd needed to while I was busy making grave-looking faces. It was pretty different from how I'd done things until now, but...maybe it would be best to learn a little more from the way *they* did things. They were the ones who knew about this world, after all—not me.

"We'll follow Troach's recon intel and explore north of the kingdom."

After I said that, Troach gave me a happy-looking grin.

"Anything else? Nothing? Last chance! All right!" Mizuho said, clapping her hands together. "The Round Table is thus concluded! Please gather in the north area of the palace as soon as you've finished your preparations!"

18

The north section of the camp, now the royal palace, was a sheer stone wall. Near its center was a fairly sizable arch-shaped aperture.

It looked old and sported noticeable wear. Something had been carved into it, but almost none of the markings were discernible.

"Mizuho, can you read this?" Troach asked, pointing at the arch.

Mizuho squinted and got close to it, but shook her head. "Fire...? Temple...? Hmm. I can't read it like this. Not when it's this worn down."

"Maybe it denotes what sort of place this is," I remarked. "There's remains of fires all over, and the pillars are tightly packed, similar to a temple."

"Similar to a temple...?" Mizuho repeated, shaking her head again. "But there's no elevator."

"...What?"

"Elevators. Used for ferrying offerings to the heavenfloors or deepfloors... Oh, but there's a chance this pillar was modeled after one..."

Mizuho fell into thought. She'd told me that storytellers did their jobs out of a love of song and entertaining, but in her case, she seemed to have taken to the work out of academic curiosity. The young woman clearly preferred discovering knowledge firsthand rather than hearing it from someone else.

The "elevators" of this world had to be different than the ones I knew about, but popping that question would just delay things even more. Instead, I cleared my throat and said, "Shouldn't we get moving?"

"Oh! Right!"

Snapping back to reality, Mizuho looked around at the assembled group. The three of the Court plus six young men and women as subordinates, and the twenty-one others, who had come to see them off.

"Everyone ended up following us anyway! Not that I don't understand, of course," Troach observed with a laugh. "Taiga, you do the honors."

"What do you mean?"

"This is the first expedition of our Great Camp Bravo Kingdom. You have to really give them a good show!"

"That's right. Though you may not be the King, you are still our foundation. Please give them a few words."

That wasn't an easy thing they were asking. With twenty-nine pairs of anticipation-filled eyes on me, anxiety settled in. What was I going to do?

"I suppose... Ahem. We're about to be heading off to a dangerous dungeon in search of food and resources. I ask that you all please stay wary of injury and move with care... Errr."

Realizing my speech was pretty crappy, I stopped. While I hadn't asked for this position of responsibility, those counting on me still deserved more inspiring words.

I brought my head up and looked to everyone again.

"To be honest... I don't know how much use I'll be to you all. I'm an ignorant outsider, and there is probably far more you could teach me than the other way around. I'm used to taking on missions with other soldiers who have the same training I do, but I have no experience living alongside folk like you who *aren't* warriors. Everything is as new to me as it is to you, if not more so. However..."

I watched for their reactions and then let myself pause for a moment. Everyone was staring at me, silently waiting.

"...we had a motto in the unit I was trained in. Who Dares Wins. When you're face-to-face with fear, and you feel like your legs might give out, the ones who can stand their ground and stay on their feet will survive and emerge victoriously. That was our ironclad rule. I swear to stand for you, the people of the Great Camp Bravo Kingdom, no matter what dangers arise. Not only have you gladly accepted an outsider as one of your own, but you've also gone so far as to make him your King. This is my way of thanking you."

The words were awkwardly spoken and came off the top of my head, but they seemed to make a more profound impression than I'd expected. No sooner had I finished than everyone present broke into cheers.

"Long live the King! Glory to Taiga!" came several significantly more excited cheers than the rest. They were coming from Troach.

I raised a hand to calm the applause; the crowd looked back at me with anticipation in their eyes, wondering what I'd say next.

"Thank you. We had another motto in my unit. This one is actually more important than the first. It goes: Check test, check test, check test. Those with only courage die quickly. Without the training to take the proper action in every situation, you will die. Therefore, I'm starting your training now."

The cheers this time were a little more confused than last time.

Admittedly, calling it training was a bit much.

We had no complex gear that needed to be inspected to ensure its operation, and I couldn't afford to expect an actual combat force out of these people. Instead, I had them do one thing—get down.

After lining up the six we'd be bringing as subordinates, I would shout "Get down!" and they would immediately drop on the spot. That was all.

I had them practice this while they were standing in a line, while we were walking, while we were carrying things, while one person was helping another, while our eyes were closed, while dizzy, and so on. The floor was stone, so if one panicked and dropped ungracefully, it was no different from tripping. This training was to make sure they would go prone safely. If they broke a bone while falling, the whole thing would be a waste. I demonstrated a few examples, using my limbs to cushion my fall and teaching them the proper way to do it, but none of them had experience with this kind of motion, so everyone had a pretty hard time. As they gradually started getting used to it, I had them place stones along the ground to rehearse the motion on less even terrain.

At first, everyone was fascinated by this and watched over the six chosen assistants, with many offering sarcastic encouragement. After realizing nothing interesting was going to happen other than them dropping prone, people dispersed. As practice continued, the enthusiasm rapidly faded from our subordinates' eyes.

"...All right, that should be enough," I stated, checking my wristwatch as the six got to their feet, breathing heavily. We couldn't afford to stay here forever, and we'd only spent an hour at most on training, but even that was probably a pretty severe experience for them all.

"Drink some water and take a rest. Once you've caught your breath, we'll set out."

"Oh, it's over?" Troach asked, looking up from organizing our equipment.

Perhaps I should've anticipated as much, but Troach took quickly to the maneuver. She'd bragged about being a "moneygrubbing burglar," but she was good. I recalled her title: Troach of the Complicated Past. I found myself slightly interested in what exactly that meant.

Mizuho, on the other hand, was a lost cause. She was too worried about her glasses to even lower herself onto the ground. And with them off, she couldn't really see her footing, either.

She moaned. "I told you this wasn't my area of expertise..."

Troach put a hand on her shoulder as she squatted down despondently. "It's fine. I'll watch your back, Mizuho."

"That only makes me *more* worried..."

"Wait, why?!"

I'd have to place Mizuho in the middle of our formation so that either Troach or I could guard her if and when danger approached.

The three of us borrowed the three best daggers in the nation as equipment. For illumination, we had our lanterns with star fragments inside. I'd refrain from using my SureFire as much as possible. I wanted to conserve its battery, and its illumination was far more potent than these stars were, so it also ran the risk of blinding my allies.

Mizuho carried several other small items, but they were all little tools she used when telling stories. By her own admission, none of them would be helpful. I wondered where her Babel bird feathers were. One had given me a pretty nasty shock the other day. However, when I thought about it more carefully, I realized they were useless quills unless there was another Visitor.

All six subordinates were given bags to carry whatever we could harvest. We'd fashioned them from bits of cloth around camp, so their sizes and shapes were all over the place.

The simple backpack Troach wore contained only the barest essentials: rope, waterskins, and the absolute last of what little preserved food we had (like dried meat scraps that tasted like tree roots when you bit into them).

I looked around at our party. Some were more nervous than others, and their initial excitement was gone.

"All right… Let's get moving, then."

Wordless nods were the only response.

At last, we took our first steps into the northern passage.

19

It felt almost like the air had changed just stepping through that arch. A chill wind crawled up us from our feet, sending shivers up our backs. The ceiling was high enough, but the sense of confinement was palpable. The rocky passage, which looked solid and sturdy at a glance, had dozens, hundreds, or perhaps even more dungeon floors piled on top of it. Not knowing when it could all come crumbling down on us was suffocating if you dwelled on it.

Troach stood at the front, followed by one subordinate, then Mizuho, then me, then the remaining five. Marching in the comparatively safe center of our group left me feeling uneasy, but it was the only way I could protect Mizuho and the rest if something happened.

I would have preferred to lead the march, eliminating dangers and then calling for the rest of the team to move up. Unfortunately, Mizuho and Troach were firmly against that idea. In their words, I still didn't understand what dangers lurked in the labyrinth. My lack of knowledge could mean failing to spot hazards in time.

I couldn't argue with them. My experience had shown that advice like this from the locals was not to be ignored. After all, they were the ones who knew about this world, not me.

When I made an unenthusiastic face about the prospect, Troach had said, *"You'll be fine. I'll be your eyes, Taiga."*

That was why Troach took point.

She took the lead, with only the one subordinate keeping close to her. There was some distance between the pair and the remainder of the party. This was to watch out for ambushes and traps. The one with Troach, a girl who never smiled, was in charge of communicating with the rear group. She was also tasked with carrying the light, and we nervously watched as the glow from her low-hanging lantern wavered up ahead.

As we continued through the old corridor, the walls and ceiling eventually gave way to bare, uneven rock. The passage itself got abruptly wider as well. I glanced up and saw the lantern's light flickering off some hanging stalactites. We had come into a natural cave.

The girl with Troach waved her lantern from side to side. It was a signal we'd decided on beforehand.

"Procession, halt," I said. Mizuho and our subordinates stopped moving. The girl in charge of communication ran back to us. Upon arrival, she delivered a short report.

"Something ahead. Lots of animal dung around."

"Okay. Everyone wait here, you included. Mizuho, with me."

"R-right away!"

With our assistants standing by, I brought Mizuho and caught up to where Troach was. She pointed ahead; I looked and saw black dollops around the cavern floor. They only increased in number as the path continued—there was too much of it to count. The hardened feces were layered on top of one another, forming an additional level on the floor. Curiously, they didn't smell very bad, perhaps since they'd dried out.

"Know what it could be, Mizuho?" I asked quietly.

Mizuho answered immediately. "Greatbats, most likely. You can find them anywhere. Exterminating them is the first priority for any Landmakers who want to expand their territory."

"Bats, eh… In my world, bat dung is a carrier of harmful diseases. What about in Million Dungeon?"

"It's the same! Word is, you can contract illnesses by touching a bat."

Thought so. I focused my gaze above where the dung was most plentiful. There, several glowing eyes stared back from between the stalactites.

"I see them there. Think we can get by without bothering them?"

"They've already noticed us. Greatbats are highly territorial. If we move nearer, they'll likely attack," Troach stated, twirling her dagger.

"Are they something we can handle, Mizuho?"

"They are somewhat troublesome since they can fly, but I've never heard of a Landmaker losing to greatbats before."

"Got it. Let's head back for now," I decided.

That earned me some surprised looks. There probably weren't many

Landmakers who would flee from these creatures. Still, perhaps knowing we were about to face an enemy, they kept quiet and followed me when I turned around.

When I got back to the five we'd left behind, I said, "Everyone, I want you to cover your noses and mouths. Can't cover our eyes, I suppose, but don't rub them even if they get itchy."

"What do you mean?"

"We're going to get rid of some greatbats, but when they flap their wings, particles of dried dung will get into the air. You risk contracting a disease if you inhale it."

The diseases in the dung of Earth bats were hazardous as well. Asthma and allergies were just the beginning. There was rabies, too, and in certain places, you could even catch Ebola hemorrhagic fever. I had no way of knowing if the same maladies existed in Million Dungeon, but if humans from my planet had made it to this world, it wasn't out of the question to think diseases had, too.

An infectious illness running rampant in our currently medical-facility-less nation could wipe us all out. Decreasing our risk of infection was a priority.

Once the bottom half of everyone's faces were covered with clothes, I continued:

"Troach and I will draw the greatbats away. All others should stay back and wait. Mizuho—"

"I can fight, too!"

"I know that. You'll be the rear line. We need you to protect the rest."

The blue-haired girl nodded, but the words *Fine, but I'm not happy about it* were written all over her face. Still, even if she was raring to go, I couldn't put her on the front line.

"Ready, Troach?"

"Yeah. Enjoy watching how cool I am, okay?"

I didn't need to look back to know Mizuho's reaction.

Troach and I drew our daggers and moved in. The lantern behind us revealed the ceiling head, and a moment later, we heard shrill shrieking, followed by a large figure appearing from between the stalactites.

A greatbat—and was it ever great! I'd imagined an animal comparable to those on Earth, with a wingspan of no more than a meter. However, this creature's was *twice* that. It was like a medium-sized dog had grown car doors. More of them followed, too, dancing through the air.

After assuming gliding positions, with more shrill squeaks, they headed straight for us. Six in all. A considerable threat if you thought of it like a pack of flying wild dogs attacking you.

"Monsters, huh?"

"What did you think they were?"

"Any tricks for them?"

"Get them on the ground, and they're ours."

No sooner had Troach and I finished our exchange than the first of the greatbats made its move. A complex maze of wrinkles lined the muzzle coming at us. I bent backward at the last moment to avoid it, stabbing my dagger into its body as it passed.

The blade pierced its soft flank, and I felt the tearing sensation through my weapon. The impact very nearly ripped the dagger out of my hand. The greatbat let out its final scream and fell to the ground.

Without a moment's delay, the next one came charging in. I reacted immediately, swinging my blade and slicing through the membrane of its wing. When it lost its balance and started to plummet at an angle, Troach finished it off from the side.

She'd already dealt with another. The group of six greatbats had been halved. Just when I thought the rest would be as easy, the enemies' movements shifted. The remaining three beasts started calling to one another from a height we couldn't reach, turning in a circle. Suddenly, they swooped past Troach and me. Their course would bring them straight to Mizuho and our subordinates.

"Get down!" I called out at once.

The training bore fruit. Our six subordinates dropped on the spot. Mizuho, however, remained standing by herself. The three bats, now with a single target, closed in…

A moment later, a *bang* echoed through the cave. I lowered myself out of reflex. It sounded like a gunshot to me, but that should've been impossible.

In Mizuho's hand was a small, conical paper tube.

A party popper, essentially. I remembered hearing last night that they frequently used gunpowder to stave off wild creatures.

It had a massive effect on the greatbats. One of them, taking the brunt of the noise, was dazed; it haphazardly spun and fell. The other two, seeming surprised, changed course as well, then ran into the stalagmites protruding from the ground.

Troach and I hurried over. Before the writhing greatbats could retake flight, we stepped on their wings to stop them from moving and slit their throats. We turned back to witness Mizuho delivering the final blow to the one that had fallen right in front of her.

She looked up and gave a smug look. "I told you I could fight, didn't I?"

"Seems you can."

I revised my opinion of Mizuho. She was by no means physically powerful, but she had other strengths that set her above and beyond ordinary people.

The difference between regular folk and Landmakers was rapidly becoming apparent. Landmakers were those who could literally *fight* for their citizens. They stood stalwart in the face of violence. Having thought that far, I had to laugh, remembering that motto from the Regiment. Who Dares Wins. This was no different.

The subordinates rose from their prone positions and cheered. It was our Court's first triumph. Nobody appeared hurt, which was a relief.

"That was so cool, Mizuho! I think I was cooler, though."

"I wasn't watching. Please do it again."

"But there's no bad guys left!"

"That's a shame."

As Troach and Mizuho bickered, I contemplated a few things.

The first was that the pair had proved surprisingly reliable. And looking down at the greatbat corpses piled on the cavern floor really drove home the second thing—I wished I had a shotgun.

It was entirely out of the question, but having a dagger as my only weapon was just so unreliable. I'd have to procure more weapons somehow.

20

The area beyond the greatbat's roost had fallen in. Upon moving along one of the walls, we found another passage that continued west. It was a natural hollow, much narrower than the first corridor, only about three meters across and high. At least, it *looked* like an organic formation. I had no reason to suspect otherwise until Troach almost dropped into an elaborately constructed pitfall.

We heard the shriek after going about two hundred meters. Troach hung from the side of the hole with only one hand. I understood why after rushing over. Her other arm was holding on to the girl in charge of communicating, who was dangling. (Her name, I'd heard, was Kanlo.)

The hole was clearly man-made. It had been constructed to come apart from the middle and drop whoever was on top of it inside. Sharpened sticks were waiting to meet you at the bottom.

"Crap, crap, I can't hold on!" groaned Troach, clenching her teeth.

The pitfall's cover, which had opened up from either side, slowly started to reset via some mechanism. The thick sheets of rock were moving in. If Troach let go, she and Kanlo were dead, and if her hand got caught in the two halves of the cover, she'd have to drop.

I swiftly checked all around the pitfall. It could have been a double trap meant to maim or kill whoever tried to help the victims. Not seeing anything of that nature, I got down on my stomach and reached for Troach's arm. I grabbed it not a moment before her fingers slipped off the edge of the hole.

"Hang on—I'll pull you up."

"Wait! Kanlo! Wrap your arms and legs around my leg! Do *not* let go!"

With help from the other subordinates, we dragged Troach and Kanlo out in a single pull. A moment later, the trap's lid shut with a dull, heavy sound.

"Phew... That woke me up. That was scary, huh, Kanlo?"

Kanlo nodded, unable to speak.

"Are you okay, Troach?" Mizuho asked worriedly.

Troach stood up and combed her hair back. "I really messed up there. Didn't notice it at all. Seems it wasn't made to trigger under the weight of only a single person, or maybe it only activates a set period after being stepped on."

I looked at the floor more closely, focusing on the area around the pitfall. You could barely see the gap in the lid now that it was closed tight. Now that was some outstanding craftsmanship—*industrial capability*, even.

Raising my head, I looked around. Troach took notice of that.

"What's wrong? You've got a look on your face."

"What is an advanced machine like this doing here...? This place looked just like a naturally formed cave."

If someone wanted to dig a pitfall, there were much simpler ways to go about it.

"They pop up sometimes—traps that don't fit in," explained Troach.

"Pop up...?"

As I struggled to puzzle that one out, Mizuho stepped in. "Do you remember what I said about the Dungeon Calamity?"

"Yeah. The dungeon formed on its own, expanded, and covered the whole world—"

As I said that, I figured it out.

"...You mean these traps aren't man-made—they were produced naturally?"

"Most likely, yes. And it isn't just the traps. This passage, the rooms, the strata—they all look constructed, but the Dungeon Calamity created the majority of them. That's why sometimes you encounter things that don't match the location."

"Is that right...?"

"Oh, but not everything, of course. Just as people have modified the labyrinth to make it into a living space, other races and monsters have rebuilt things to make it easier for them as well."

"But there's also a lot of unexpected traps that come out of the environment nearby. The magical ones are even more of a pain to deal with."

"Huh," I grunted. This would be troublesome. I'd have to expand my concept of what these devices could be.

Traps were always annoying to handle—just by making someone suspect one might be around, you could hamper their actions. A true master of snares and tripwires could manipulate the actions of entire enemy forces based on where they did or didn't lay their snares. Fighting back meant predicting how the one who'd set the things thought.

According to Troach and Mizuho, however, Million Dungeon's pitfalls and other hazards hadn't been set with any strategy in mind.

"Ahh, here we go. This is what I stepped on." Troach had located the trap's switch. One of the rocks on the floor was actually a pressure plate. With a piece of red chalk, she drew a circle around it.

"Be careful you don't step on this, everyone!"

There was another switch on the opposite side of the hole, nicely symmetrical, and the pitfall would open no matter which was activated. It seemed like we'd be fine if we avoided them, so we crossed over the cover one at a time.

From then on, we were even more careful as we proceeded. What's more, we were carrying meat from the six greatbats we'd slain. Even after draining the blood, the bodies were cumbersome, which slowed the pace of the subordinates carrying them.

It would have been easier to leave them there and pick them up on the way back, but when I suggested as much, Mizuho and Troach told me other creatures would snatch the food up without leaving so much as bones behind. Million Dungeon seemed to be a place that punished even the slightest missteps.

When I first heard we'd be eating the greatbat meat, I was surprised. Apparently, though, it was standard fare in Million Dungeon. And come to think of it, there were regions on Earth where people ate them, too. A friend who went to Papua New Guinea said they were surprisingly delicious, though you had to cook them well to eliminate the dangers.

As I was busy pondering the taste of greatbat meat, the passage's appearance changed once again. The walls of exposed, sturdy boulder gave way to dirt, and we began to see things that looked like small, white beards hanging out of the ceiling. Plant roots.

Before long, we set foot into a new room.

It was spacious and circular. The walls and ceiling were all covered end to end with ivy. Under our feet was a stretch of green. The floor rose slightly toward the center, forming a hill about a meter high.

Atop that mound was a tree. A beautiful, gracefully shaped, leafy thing that stretched up and out toward the dome-shaped ceiling...

"Hey, everyone, we found a tree!" Troach called from over her shoulder.

Cheers sounded. With timber that big, we'd have enough fuel to last us for a while. We couldn't chop down the entire thing, but harvesting its branches would be more than enough for now. We could probably use the ivy on the walls, too. The subordinates set to work, each taking out axes and billhooks.

We entered the room carefully and proceeded with caution.

This was the first time I'd felt something soft underfoot since coming to this world. I'd heard about plants growing in the dungeon before, but it still struck me as mysterious.

That was when I realized how quiet Mizuho had gotten.

"Something wrong?"

"Something...isn't right, at least."

Mizuho frowned and scanned the chamber. I'd been paying attention, too, naturally, for any signs of change, yet all seemed quiet at the moment, and aside from the sound of our feet parting the grass, the only thing to be heard was the rustling of leaves.

I looked back up at the great tree atop the hill. Amid the swaying branches, I spotted several red fruits. They looked a lot like apples.

"Mizuho, is that fruit edible?" I asked, holding the lantern up toward one in particular. Mizuho squirted up at the treetop...

She and I realized what was amiss at nearly the same time.

"There's no stars!" Mizuho cried sharply.

Plants weren't supposed to grow without light. A tree like that would never have flourished in a room without any stars.

What's more, how was the tree swaying without any wind?

"Get down!" I bellowed just as the thing began to move more. Its long, undulating branches split the air like whips, slamming into Troach, who was in the lead.

"Agh!"

With a pained cry, Troach was knocked away. I jumped out in front, grabbed Mizuho, and took us both down to the ground just as a big tendril mowed over our heads.

The ground was unexpectedly soft and damp. This was no grass—it was a massive sheet of moss!

A split ran through the tree's trunk, and from inside, large eyeballs appeared. Sharp teeth now lined a spot that had looked like a cavity. It must have been waiting for us to get close. Abandoning all pretense, the tree-thing bent its trunk and swung all its huge branches.

Mizuho shouted the monster's name. "It's a treant!"

I stood on the moss, then helped Mizuho up as I turned around, meaning to order the subordinates behind us to withdraw. However, I then saw something that made me doubt my eyes. The ivy all over the walls was moving on its own. It was obviously making a clear effort to seal the entrance we'd come through.

"Mizuho, what *are* those?"

The young woman widened her eyes when she saw what I was pointing to. Then she moaned.

"Bloodsucking kudzu vines. If you get close, they'll wrap around you. Be careful!"

It seemed we'd been led right onto the dinner table of a bunch of man-eating plants.

21

Large branches creaked like drawn bowstrings and barreled down all at once.

I shoved Mizuho aside and threw myself in the other direction. The limbs slammed into the ground between us, scattering moss and earth.

"Run! Distance yourself from those branches!" I shouted, bounding to my feet before dashing the opposite way as Mizuho. "Over here! Monster! Look at me!" I roared, trying to draw its attention.

The treant, however, simply glanced at me with one of its multiple eyeballs before immediately returning its attention to Mizuho. Over and over, it brought its limbs up and swung them back down at her.

"Eek! Ack! Ahhh!"

As Mizuho scrambled away at a half crawl, the branch tips gouged out chunks of the floor, sending them flying. If the treant had been just a little faster, Mizuho would have been torn to shreds.

Meanwhile, the bloodsucking kudzu vines weren't just creeping along the walls. They had lowered to the floor and were steadily moving in. That put us in a pincer between the treant in the middle and the vines on the walls. One subordinate's ankle touched a tendril, which quickly wrapped itself around his ankle and brought him to the ground. More vines coiled around his body from all directions as he cried out.

On the opposite side of the room, Troach, having been knocked away, was holding her head and trying to stand up. Several vines had already closed in on her from behind.

"Troach, behind you!"

"...Huh?"

She turned around, noticing it, but it was too late. The ivy wrapped itself around her limbs all at once, dragging her down as she struggled.

"Agh, dammit!"

She used the dagger in her hand to slice at the ivy. It would withdraw, as though flinching away, but then other vines would move in to entangle her a moment later.

Having recovered from the shock of our initial encounter, I tried to get the complete picture of the situation. All our subordinates were desperately trying to escape the bloodsucking kudzu vines. The treant was tenaciously whipping its branches down at Mizuho. Thankfully, she was keeping out of its range. She finally stood up, but she couldn't retreat to the wall because of the ivy at her feet. Troach was battling the bloodthirsty tendrils herself, cursing all the while.

With Mizuho having fled, the treant turned its attention to me at last. Several large, unfurled branches struck from either side, and I dodged at the last moment.

Threat priority was the bloodsucking vines first, then the treant second. The treant wasn't moving, so we could simply stay out of its reach. We needed to clear the walls of ivy.

Having settled on a course of action, I ran to our subordinates, who were steadily being entrapped. They naturally hoped that I, dashing over, would help them, but I didn't have time to rescue all six. I picked up two hand axes they'd dropped, then tossed one to Mizuho, who was surrounded by tendrils.

"Cut the ivy! Don't get close to the treant!" I instructed before sprinting across the room toward Troach. The monstrous tree wasn't swift enough to keep up with my movements. Still, the sheer momentum of the branches slamming the floor behind me was enough to send chills down my spine.

When I reached Troach, I raised my ax and started hacking away at any floor-crawling plants I could see. The hatchet was crude, its rivets loose. It could barely be called a proper weapon. Still, it was well suited for this purpose. There was a *lot* of ivy, and it tried to twine around me, but I ignored them as long as they didn't restrict my arm movements and worked on saving Troach instead.

Eventually, we'd cut through most of the vines holding Troach down, and she peeled off the rest on her own.

"Sorry—and thanks."

"No worries. Can you move?"

"Hurts a little, but…yeah," she replied, scrunching her face up. That initial hit had been a severe one, and bloodsucking kudzu vines did just that—they drained the blood of their victims. Several thorns protruding from the ivy had stuck me, too. Individual pieces couldn't drain all that much, it seemed, but they would be a threat in numbers.

Troach, noticing my gaze, annoyedly added, "We can worry about me after we cut our way out of here. We have to save her now, right? I'm going ahead!"

No sooner had the words left her mouth than she was running toward the treant. It lashed out with its branches, but not a single one landed. I watched for the right timing and followed after her.

"Mizuho! Sorry for the wait!"

Troach ran to Mizuho's side as the storyteller was fighting desperately against the bloodsucking vines.

"Troach! Are you okay?"

"Perfectly fine!"

I caught up as well, joining the work of rescuing our subordinates. With the three of us swinging axes and billhooks, even the numerous bloodsucking kudzu vines couldn't keep up. Before long, the ivy gave up on its prey and withdrew to the walls, leaving behind a substantial quantity of dead tendrils.

That was one danger handled. We were safe as long as we were out of the treant's attack range. What's more, all this gathered ivy meant we had a fair supply of fuel and a good resource for making tools.

Unfortunately, our luck came to an end when I saw the treant, which was atop the hill, pull its own roots out of the ground and start slinking toward us.

Seeing a man-eating tree move closer was both surreal and terrifying. I'd wished I had a shotgun when we ran into those greatbats, but now I couldn't help thinking how nice it would be if I had a flamethrower. Not that I'd ever touched one back in the Regiment, but still...

"Didn't think it'd be able to walk."

Mizuho's eyes were wide, too. "I've never personally seen one do it, either..."

The thick tree roots moved across the earth like hoes as the treant approached. If it got any closer and swung its branches, we'd have casualties for sure. We'd have to disable it—

A hard outer skin guarded the enemy's entire body. Probably best to assume just hacking at it wouldn't have any effect. However, since it had eyes and a mouth, it was reasonable to trust that it possessed internal organs. In other words, the only way to take it down would be to deal a fatal wound to its exposed eyeballs or its vital parts through its oral cavity.

Despite my efforts to attract its attention earlier, it had ignored me. That suggested its vision was poor, and it couldn't hear anything. What sense was it using to find prey, then?

...*Smell!* It was discerning creatures' locations by scent. In a dark place like Million Dungeon, that seemed the best option.

I scooped up a piece of fresh meat on the ground—a greatbat corpse—and hurled it in the treant's path. It reacted immediately. The movement was probably reflexive; all its branches moved in tandem, snatching the greatbat corpse as it was in the air.

"Aim for the eyes!" I shouted to Troach as I dashed up to the treant, lobbing my hand ax into its wide-open mouth as hard as I could. With a *pop*, its mouth closed. That must have been involuntary, too. Vivid-red fluid came flowing out from between its locked fangs, so I could tell I'd wounded it.

The next thing I did was ram my dagger deep into the eye attached to the side of its mouth. It felt like I'd stabbed a giant grape. Tree sap came gushing out, its color reminiscent of blood. It smelled sweet, though, almost like concentrated fruit juice.

On the other side of the trunk, Troach split through another eyeball. After abandoning the greatbat corpse, the treant tried to attack, but its hard branches were covered in firm, inflexible bark. The monster couldn't injure anything that got too close. The treetop leaves smacking us in the back did as much as those white-birch sauna whisks you struck your body with in Scandinavian saunas.

The treant wriggled its thick roots in rage, but Troach and I clung to the bough and endured it until its movements faltered. The flow of sap waned as well. Troach and I backed off as its branches, once wildly flailing, all dropped limp and finally drooped to the ground.

After a moment's pause, the room was filled with cheering.

"We did it..."

Troach fell backward into a sitting position. Mizuho ran up to us and asked, "Are you okay?!"

"Yeah." I wiped the spray of sap off my face, then did the same for my dagger before sheathing it. The fluid flowing from the treant's remains dyed the moss red and melted into the earth. It looked like all threats had been neutralized.

"Let's see to the wounded," I said. "Is anyone hurt?"

A check revealed that everyone had some scrapes and bruises, some larger than others, but most of them were from the bloodsucking kudzu vine thorns. Small punctures, a bit of shed blood, the congestion from having been squeezed. It was a stroke of luck that nobody had suffocated.

Troach was still the one who had taken the most damage. Her bruises and abrasions from the treant's attack were severe.

"Could you maybe stop moving? I can't help you like that."

Troach writhed in displeasure as Mizuho tried to check her injuries. "Ow! That hurts! It's nothing major! Anyway, I'm the Attendant here, so it's supposed to be *my* job to fix everyone up!"

"Just be quiet and stay still."

Still, the only medical supplies we had on hand were some pieces of cloth that had been sterilized in a pot. All we could do was wash the wounds in clean water and cover them up. I shuddered, belatedly realizing how dangerous a place we'd ventured into. There'd been little other choice, but things could have easily gone far worse for us.

I was worried about the puncture wounds from the bloodsucking kudzu vines, but Mizuho set me at ease a little, telling me she'd never heard of them being poisonous. It was a good thing we'd boiled water before setting out. The number one scariest thing in the wild was a bacterial infection. Simply not cleaning an injury caused the risk of disease to skyrocket.

I'd begun to learn firsthand how dangerous the labyrinth was. The threats we encountered here weren't all of a size that humans could handle. We managed to fight our way through this one with some desperate maneuvers, but challenging a tree like that without any real weapons was insanity. This wasn't *Minecraft*.

"I'm sorry—this is all I have."

Mizuho took a salve from her own things and applied it to Troach's bruise.

"Ow, ow... Are you sure? That stuff seems valuable."

"It's meant for the bruises and scrapes that kids get, so... It's more just for ease of mind," Mizuho admitted, wrapping the cloth over the balm and causing Troach to cry out again.

I had Mizuho show me the salve. It smelled of fragrant perfume. It wouldn't seep into the skin when applied. Mizuho explained that she'd used it since she was young. I had no way of analyzing it, but it didn't look harmful, at least.

After finishing our first aid, we took our meal so that we could rest. We split up what little preserved food we had, relishing the meat's flavor, even though the stuff was as hard and dry as boot soles.

We'd brought some embers from the campfire in case we had to make camp while exploring. I'd wrapped a few glowing sparks in some small woodchips, covered that with a bag made of rough fabric, then put it into a metal container with a hole in it for ventilation. The air coming in through that aperture would keep it burning slowly, which allowed us to walk around with still-living embers. Having ready-to-use sparks on hand was convenient. Firemaking from scratch was a pain, to say the least.

I started a small campfire using dried kudzu ivy and dead sticks that had fallen to the treant's roots. I stood some branches up as supports, then hung a small billycan over the flame. In my survival training in the Regiment, they'd first had us make our own billycans out of empty soda cans. They were handy tools, useful for both boiling water and cooking.

While heating the water, I came to a decision. I stood up and went over to the remains of the treant. I'd just remembered the fruits that had been growing on it. Cutting one of them off with my dagger, I found it to be softer and more rubbery than expected. It felt less like an apple and more like a single plucked grape or berry made much bigger. I cut it open and rubbed its juices on the inside of my wrist. It didn't seem to cause itchiness or a rash.

"You're not really gonna eat that, are you?" Troach asked dubiously. "That fruit was growing on a man-eating tree."

"No—we can't afford to eat it and be poisoned."

"Right? Phew."

"We'll test it after getting back to our nation. If you have extra room, put it with the rest of your things."

"……"

Starving and stranded people often made the mistake of risking it all on any animal or plant that looked edible. Unfortunately, the natural world was filled with things indigestible by humans. Many were also toxic.

However, we lacked much of any kind of food in our country. If we found anything that looked the least bit consumable, we needed to test its safety as much as possible. Perhaps that was something I would be better at than a native, being a visitor to Million Dungeon without any preconceptions.

The water had started to boil, so I took out a tree root that supposedly had a taste if you bit into it from our stash of preserved food. I set it in the billycan and boiled it for a few minutes. When the water became tinged with color, I took the makeshift pot off the heat, waited for it to cool, and gave it a sip.

"What are you doing over there, Taiga?"

"Trying to make tea."

"Did it work?"

I let myself taste the liquid in my mouth for a moment before answering Mizuho's question.

"...It has a taste."

I passed around this tea, of which I could only say it had a taste, and we drank. When the billycan made it back to me, I took it and downed the remaining liquid. Then, throwing the tree-root grounds "with a taste" into my mouth, I stood up.

"Break time is over. Let's get to work."

22

With blades in hand, we harvested the wood. There was so much ivy that had been cut down during the battle as well that collecting it all was an entire job by itself. Landmakers or not, we never would have finished without everyone's help.

The remaining bloodsucking kudzu vines had crawled up the walls and curled up near the ceiling. I considered exterminating them but decided against it. We didn't have the time, and if we let them grow, we could harvest them again.

We could use the ivy as is for makeshift ropes to tie what we gathered together, too. A little elbow grease, and they'd make even better tools. Once we returned, I'd have to ask that executioner about it.

We didn't have the tools or workforce to put the entirety of the treant to good use. Regretfully, we'd have to leave the better part of it here. Still, we cut off all the bark and wood we were able to and packed them into our things.

Taking three straight branches, I shaved off the skin and fixed the dagger onto their tip. With that, I'd made a spear. Able to be handled even in a narrow passage, it was at most the height of a person, but its reach and power were still nothing to laugh at.

Estimating how much we could carry back, I gathered lumber until I couldn't hold any more. As I looked up, figuring that would be enough, I saw Mizuho and Troach looking down at their feet atop the hill. The subordinates working nearby had gathered around them, too.

What's going on?

I climbed up the hill. Mizuho turned to me and said, "Taiga, we found something…"

What they were looking at was a large hole that had opened at the top of the hill. It was where the treant had pulled its roots from; the earth seemed to have fallen in and formed a pit. Several white stone fragments were buried around the crater, making it look like a gravestone or monument.

"There's a cave down there. Look."

Troach hung a lantern onto the spear I'd just made and lit up the pit. She was right—under the hole seemed to be an empty, open space. It was partially obscured by the dirt that had fallen from above, but the stone flooring was visible. It was about five or six meters down.

"What should we do? If we descend a floor, we might find more stuff."

I thought for a moment. With everyone safe and having found the meat and wood we were after, it was logically unnecessary to take on any more risk.

"Do stronger monsters appear the lower you go, or something like that?"

Mizuho shook her head at my question. "Maybe if you went very, very deep into the dungeon to where the Deep Ones live, but there's generally no difference in threats whether you go up or down."

"And I hear if you go up, you find strange things called High Risers loitering around," Troach added. "Million Dungeon is perilous in any direction."

"...All right. I'll go and check."

"Huh?"

"Wait, you?"

I nodded at the surprised girls. "We have too many things for us all to investigate. It'll be a lighter trip if I take it alone."

"You're not wrong, but if you want a scout, I'm your girl—"

"No, you're already wounded. We'll need everyone up here to pull me out in case something goes wrong."

"But…"

"You stay here. Protect Mizuho and the others. I'll be right back."

Troach scratched her neck for a moment, then sighed. "Okay, fine. You better bring me back at least one souvenir."

Her face fraught with concern, Mizuho said, "Taiga, it's true that moving one stratum won't necessarily increase the threat. But it's common for monsters of similar strength to make their homes near each other. We don't know what's waiting for you down there. Please be very careful, and if you sense anything at all out of the ordinary, come back."

"Sure thing. I'll be cautious."

I took the rope and tied one end of it to the treant's corpse. Dropping my bag of ivy next to the hole, I put a thick layer of cloth down over the top of it to ensure the tether wouldn't wear away the edge of the opening.

I wrapped the cord around one of my thighs at an angle like the lower-right part of the letter *N*, and then with the upper-left curve around my opposite shoulder, I let the rest of the rope hang behind me. In this state, I could descend slowly by unraveling as I went.

"I'll only be gone for a moment," I assured, starting to rappel down to the lower floor.

The pit was barely two meters wide, but it wasn't a hindrance as long as I went down slowly. I'd done this thousands of times in the Regiment. Even without rappelling gear that had pulleys and a brake attached, if I messed up on a tiny descent like this, they'd force me to return to duty.

The wall changed from earth to stone. The lantern at my hip illuminated the floor below. No movement.

Descending the last three meters without a foothold, I landed on the ground. I heard nothing moving and took that to mean I hadn't set off any traps. Removing the rope from my body and looking up, I could see Mizuho's and Troach's silhouettes at the edge of the hole. I unhooked the lantern from my waist and swung it side to side to tell them I was safe. Then I hung the light on the end of my spear as Troach had done.

I moved the weapon around to check whether my surroundings were safe. The stone room was about six meters square. On one of the walls was a metal door. Its surface was rusted and beat-up. In the opposite corner of the room were some miscellaneous items piled up in a disorderly fashion, appearing to have been blown here by the wind.

Illuminating them with the lantern, I found some things in the garbage that were still usable—a sword free of rust, a glass container, and a large pot. I hadn't exactly struck gold, but all these things would help our Great Camp Bravo Kingdom.

As I drew near the pile, I suddenly blinked, sensing something out of place. I thought I'd just glimpsed a shimmering outline around it.

There it was again. It was almost as though there was a watery surface between the heap and me, with ripples spreading through midair...

I thrust my spear's tip in front of me. No doubt about it, something was here. A filmlike substance was floating above the ground, reflecting my lantern's light. It had something of a roundness to it, and no sooner had it withdrawn from where my spear pointed as if in displeasure than it approached me along the ground like water...

A moment later, I was nearly drowning.

I had no idea what had happened. A liquid surface had suddenly appeared and engulfed me. I paddled in desperation, getting my head into the air. The stuff immediately followed, trying to smother my face. Whatever it was, it moved just like a creature might.

No. That was just it. This *was* a creature!

It wasn't liquid, but an almost jellylike substance. It bounced and shook as it tried to swallow me. The thing's exterior was made of a thin coating that provided resistance against my thrusts.

"Taiga?! What happened?!" Mizuho's voice echoed down from above. She must have heard the commotion.

I shouted, "Some kind of clear blob is attacking me! It's trying to drown—"

The monster in question held down my head and pulled me back under.

With my spear, I stabbed through the film, and when my face next emerged, I heard Mizuho cry, "It's a slime! It should have a core in the middle! Stab—"

The creature moved around me, dragging me back in.

A core? Dammit...

I cracked my eyes open and searched for something fitting the description. The lantern had been pulled in with me, providing faint visibility. If I hadn't been about to drown, I would have called the sight *surreal.*

Several items of trash had sunk into the slime. What I thought had been lying on the ground had actually been embedded inside its body. That meant this thing drowned anyone foolish enough to let their curiosity get the better of them, then ate them. Fools like me...

The slime fluids had more resistance than water, and I needed every ounce of strength just to move my limbs. To make matters worse, I was engulfed while fully clothed. My breath *and* stamina would run out within moments. In desperation, I looked for something that might be a core, like Mizuho had said. But I couldn't see anything like that anywhere.

Finally, as I was just about to give myself up for dead, I spotted between pieces of trash a green orb that looked like a ball with most of the air sucked out of it. Translucent, it had fluid-filled tubes strung along its interior. That was it!

With the last of my energy, I paddled through the water to get close, shoved my hand into the pile of rubbish, and grabbed hold of the slime's core. I tried to crush it, but it simply changed shape in my hand; it didn't feel like I'd done any damage to it.

I thought I remembered Mizuho telling me to stab it. Groping around for any nearby trash, I found a rocky fragment. When I pushed one of its sharp edges against the thing and heaved, the core split, mixing its green into the surrounding liquid.

Suddenly, with a hard splashing noise, the slime's body collapsed. The now-lifeless fluid spread across the floor, slamming both the garbage it had absorbed and my body onto the ground. A moan like a dying dog escaped my throat as I struggled to inhale.

"Taiga! I'll be right there, so don't die!" Troach's voice came from the top of the pit.

Coughing, I answered, "I'm fine... I handled it."

"...Really?"

"All clear. No need to come down."

I picked up my spear and stood. It looked like a supersized water balloon had popped. My skin tingled, and my eyes stung, too. I popped open the cork on my water pouch and dumped the contents over my head, washing off as much of the bodily fluid clinging to my skin as I could.

What a terrifying creature that was. Once it had you inside, anyone without much endurance would immediately suffocate. The slime likely digested prey over a long period. Consuming nonorganic material seemed to serve two purposes: to lure prey and to protect its core, its only weak point.

I collected myself, then started gathering up the items scattered about the floor. I threw everything of worth into a bag, and once I finally tried to close it back up, I noticed that the rock shard that had been lying with the other discarded objects was faintly glowing. Closer inspection revealed that its surface was clouded, riddled with many scratches, but there was definitely light coming from within. The stone was also warm to the touch.

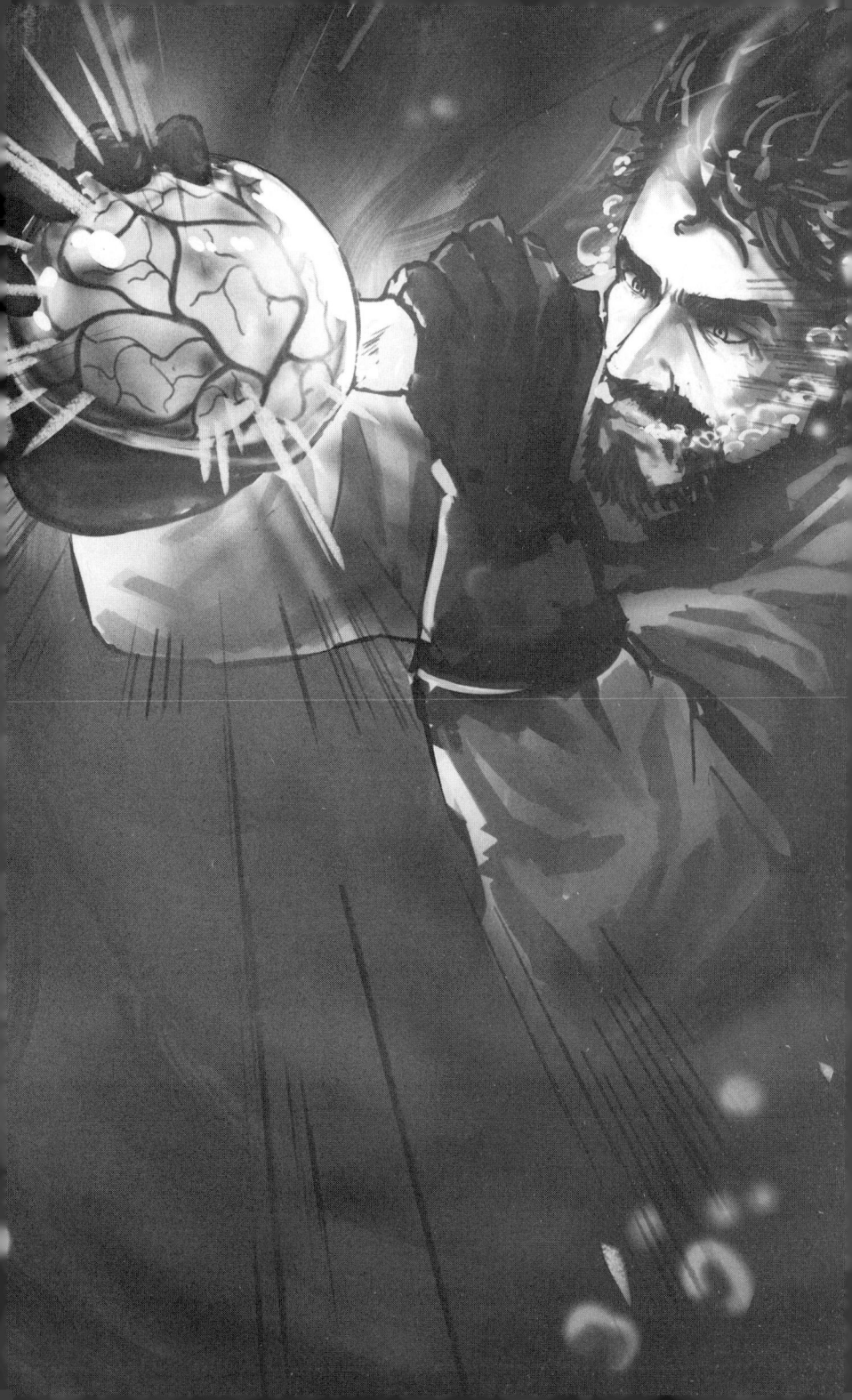

This must have been what they called a star fragment.

It was a good bit bigger than what was in my lantern. I wondered if polishing it might increase its brilliance. If it did, that would make almost drowning worth it.

Tossing the star fragment into my sack, I called up to the top of the pit, "I'm sending my bag up first. Could you pull it up?"

"Any good souvenirs?"

"I believe so."

I tied the pack to the rope, and off it went.

In the meantime, I went to check the other noteworthy thing in the room: the door. Inspection revealed it to be made of iron. Had the acidic slime rusted it?

I pressed my ear to the floor to listen for any nearby sounds. There was a distinct, if distant, low rumbling. I could only guess at its source. It could have been the legions of Hell having an assembly, and it could have been a subway car passing through the dungeon. Or maybe it was the wind echoing from the Great Fracture. I had far too little experience in Million Dungeon to figure out which.

Giving up, I stood and started investigating the door. There was no knob attached to this side. Maybe it had rusted off. After some trial and error to get the thing open, the rusted nails holding in the frame's hinges popped out—and the door fell away from the room I was in.

Gong......................
   gong....................
     gong......................
       ong.......................
         ong.......................
           ng.......................
             ....
               ....

The sound reverberated like a temple bell, echoing as the darkness swallowed it back up. I stiffened and waited for something else to happen, but even after the lingering noise faded, my surroundings were dead quiet.

I held up my lantern, peered through the opening, and abruptly found myself caught off guard. Ahead was an enormously expansive hall. It was made of stone, and its ceiling was so high that I couldn't see it.

Several doors were set into the walls. Judging by the thick dust and dense spiderwebs, nobody had been this way in some time. The end of the hall was too distant for my light, but I did spy the dim outlines of staircases with railings, walkways around atria on upper floors, and bridges that spanned the gaps across the openings.

I seemed to have found a doorway into an even larger portion of the labyrinth. Had I been an explorer, I'd have been beside myself in excitement, but unfortunately, I had more pressing matters.

Either way, going farther than this with my current equipment would be suicidal.

I lowered the lantern. This was probably a good time to wrap up today's expedition.

I went back to the pit and called up, "We're pulling out. Lower the rope again for me!"

23

When we returned to our nation, we were met with shouts and cheering.

"Three cheers for the Great Camp Bravo Kingdom!"

"Long live the King! Er, the King's representative!"

"Glory to the Ninja! Eternal glory to Taiga the Special!"

Their adulations were somewhat odd, but our first expedition had been a great success regardless. We'd accomplished our objective without a single casualty and managed to get back with more than we'd expected.

Immediately, we put some of the bloodsucking kudzu ivy into the campfire. The glowing embers took no time at all to burst into a bright-red blaze. Still, there was no time to rest upon our homecoming. I built several more fires, since we only had one, then divided up the fuel and assigned citizens to tend to each.

Thankfully, having watched me from the start, the people were quick to learn. As I was able to entrust more and more tasks to others, it looked like I wouldn't have to worry about managing the fires anymore, which was good.

The greatbats we'd brought back were butchered expertly. They hung one from its legs, and I watched their cutting process with keen interest. They stripped off the skin and washed it with water. Doubtless, it would be made into tanned leather later. It seemed they'd be able to put the wing membranes to practical use, too.

Given how large the creatures were, we gathered quite a bit of meat from them. And then, as if it was the natural thing to do, every citizen in the nation came together around the fire for a celebratory feast. Though it was simple, greatbat meat roasted over the campfire was delicious to our empty stomachs, and a few people even broke down in tears. Complaints quickly started about not having any alcohol, but I had that tea from earlier, so I was fine for now.

Nightfall brought a chill with it, but on this night, at least, the faces of all those nestled together and sleeping around the now numerous campfires in the "palace" looked to be at peace.

Starting the next day, we began the organization and classification of what we'd gathered.

From the greatbat meat, we took anything not immediately edible and smoked it. First, we cut it into thin slices, then laid them atop a shelf made of branches and heated them from underneath. We used a blanket for the smoking area. The vapors did grow pungent, but that would also serve to keep the bugs away.

As for the first campfire, we stacked more stones around it, transforming it into a turtle-shell-shaped hearth. My survival teacher in the Regiment had called this type of oven a Yukon stove. You wouldn't make one unless you planned on staying in one spot for a long time, so this was the first time I'd actually constructed one myself.

We filled the spaces between the piled-up stones with mud taken from the river, then laid a large, flat rock on the top. The countertop obviously served as a cooking stove, but we could also place food directly on it and use it as a hot plate, which broadened our culinary possibilities considerably. We'd turned the pot the slime had swallowed onto its side and buried it inside the stonework. This way, it would act as an oven.

"Which I will leave to you," I told Potesara. "You'll need it for meal preparation, right?"

The man was more grateful than I'd expected. Looking like he was about to cry from raw emotion, the former innkeeper said, "Taiga, we all owe you our lives. I'm going to rebuild my inn right here. Any food you order will be on the house."

"Ah right, well, thank you."

As long as I'd lived, I'd had few opportunities to express my thanks to someone's face, so my response was a stammered one. Then, realizing something, I asked, "Just the food? Not the drink?"

Potesara answered with a solemn look, "Booze is the business. Still, for you, the first round will be free."

We considered trying to make a second stove, but we held off, leaving it aside for future thought. I had thought Savakan's smithing job would need one, too, but even with my survival knowledge, I didn't have the know-how to understand what sort of equipment was needed for heating and striking metal. When I asked her about it, she said she actually needed a *lot* of fuel to really get the furnace going, so we carried it over as a future problem.

"It's fortunate that we're near a river," Savakan remarked. "Smithing uses a lot of water. If it was up to me, I'd put a furnace right by the stream."

"I'll keep that in mind."

For the time being, Savakan requested a job repairing broken pots and sharpening dulled blades. She claimed the campfire heat would be enough for that.

And my big souvenir for her was the door in that room where the slime had attacked me. The outside was rusted, but the other side was fine. If you took off the rust, it was a perfectly usable hunk of metal. She was overjoyed and started thinking right away about how to use it.

Still, it was a heavy door, so it'd taken a lot of work putting ropes around it and hauling it out of the pit, but once we had it up, we could also employ it as a sled to put our things on, making our return easier. (For getting across the pitfall, we removed the luggage and turned the door on its side, passing it along the wall so as not to trip the switches.) Next time we went, I wanted to have a similar device—preferably one with wheels on it.

As for the executioner (they called him Naaham the Merciful), his eyes lit up when he saw the bundles of bloodsucking kudzu vines. He informed me that by stripping off the skin, washing it with water, and weaving it together, he'd be able to make a strong rope. Additionally, he was accustomed to handling blades, so I had him work with Savakan to maintain and restore metal objects. Savakan gave the executioner an oddly wide berth, and Naaham seemed none too pleased to be polishing pots and pans, but after a few hours, they were freely yelling back and forth at each other while working, so I decided all was well.

The wood we took from the treant was used both as fuel and to make personal tools—we quickly started to run out of it. The people of Million Dungeon, in general, were good with their fingers; they'd make little items for themselves, and they'd fix broken ones rather than throwing them away. That was probably because of our current situation of scarcity.

I personally checked whether the fruit taken from the treant was safe. Whenever you first ran across new edible vegetation in a survival situation, you always had to test it. The process typically went like this.

First, you'd break the fruit or plant apart and rub its juice against the inside of your wrist. After fifteen minutes, the spot should be checked to ensure nothing unusual occurred.

Following that, the next step was to place a tiny piece of the fruit or plant in your mouth and wait five minutes without chewing it. If there was no issue, bite it. So long as it wasn't incredibly bitter or otherwise irritating, you'd then drink only the juice and spit the rest out.

After eight hours, if nothing strange happened to your body, you'd take about half a spoonful of it and then wait another eight hours.

If there were still no problematic symptoms, you'd eat a handful and wait twenty-four hours. After that, you could assume the produce was fit to eat.

That was the long and short of it. The test took the better part of two days—an arduous trial when starving. Plus, the symptoms of certain toxic foods only manifested over long periods of ingestion. You could never be too sure.

The treant fruit was fairly sour with a tinge of sweetness. It wasn't astringent, so its flavor resembled that of a wild berry—which was just what it looked like. That it was tasty didn't seem odd, since an appealing fruit would attract more prey. Nothing abnormal happened to me physically, but I did feel as though my bowels had loosened. The safest way to eat this was to cook it to eliminate the enzymes and make it into jam. I entrusted the fruit, which looked somewhat shriveled after two days, to a citizen good at cooking, making sure to mention the safety aspect.

Troach showed an aversion to consuming fruit from a man-eating plant, but after asking several others, I discovered that her viewpoint wasn't commonplace. It was probably because that treant almost ate her. Then again, after I'd gotten up out of the pit soaking wet, Troach had told me that if you slew a slime the right way, it could be prepared as food. Then she scolded me for not having done so.

I was fine with having ruined it. If even a little of myself had ended up in that slime, I didn't want to partake of it. Nor did I want to feed that to anyone else.

Thinking about it, I realized that among the spoils from the slime, there had been a usable blade and several pieces of jewelry that I'd just thrown into the bag without thinking. We'd put everything functional to immediate use, then saved the jewelry in case we had an opportunity to sell it for money. After considering ways to store the valuables, I decided to leave them in Troach's hands.

"What?! You sure you want me to handle this?!" she exclaimed upon seeing me hand her the pouch containing a golden ring, a silver anklet, and a gemstone necklace. We were standing in an isolated corner of the palace.

"I doubt anyone would be more suited for the task than you," Mizuho replied in an ironic tone.

"Umm, you know who I am, right? Formerly a thief—"

"And would anyone think to steal jewels from the nation's number one thief?"

"Aw, you're making me blush... No, wait. I mean, you trust me not to make off with them?"

"Where would you run? We at least have a little faith in you," admitted Mizuho.

"Mizuho...!" Troach, tears in her eyes, tried to hug the girl.

However, Mizuho smoothly stepped out of the way. "Please don't come any closer to me."

"But why?!"

"More importantly, Taiga, we shall need to decide what to do with the territory we've acquired," Mizuho said earnestly, ignoring Troach.

"Territory?"

"I'm referring to the rooms we've taken control of. Our country has the right to annex both the greatbat cave and the treant hill."

"Is that how it works?"

"It is customary in Million Dungeon that any nation that has taken control of a room in the dungeon has the right to decide whether to add it to their domain. Of course, should the nation grow larger, it would cost more money to administer it, so there is no hard rule saying we *must* take it... However, in our case, I believe it's best we do. At present, our nation has no facilities apart from the palace."

"Understood. If we did take it on as new territory, how would we put it to use?"

"I think we should leave the treant hill as it is for agriculture. The soil there is rich, and if we place the star you retrieved from the slime on the ceiling, it will be enough to grow crops."

That item I'd grabbed hadn't been a star fragment, but an actual star. After returning and polishing it, it had suddenly begun to shine much more brightly, almost blindingly, as though it had just remembered that was what it was supposed to do. It was currently hanging on the support beam next to the first campfire we'd made, illuminating the palace. Of course, it was only bright in the daytime; it darkened at night.

"What should we do with the bloodsucking kudzu?" I asked. "If it reaches out again, we won't be able to farm. Or should we just make a field of them…?"

"It would be a waste to plant it on such good soil. And if we leave them to crawl on the stone walls, it will mean more insects and animals coming in to steal things… I think we'll need to cut them all down and replant them elsewhere."

"Hey," Troach cut in, "if we're gonna make a farm there, wouldn't that mean you'd have to go through the greatbat cave to get to it? That means we need to improve the cave on the way, too, right?"

"It does. What shall we do with that space…? Should we build Savakan a smithing workshop?"

"I asked her, and she said a spot near water would be better."

"Isn't this palace the closest spot to water in our nation?" Troach inquired.

"Maybe we should take the chance and move the palace," I suggested.

"To the cave?" Mizuho questioned.

"I don't know yet…"

"Well, let's try and think of something. Until then, shall we put up some torches or something to at least light the way to the farmland?"

"It's so dirty in there, though. All that greatbat crap everywhere…"

Troach's remark gave me an idea. "If we need to improve that cave anyway… Can we collect the droppings?"

"Huh?"

"Pick up the poop?!"

As they gaped in disbelief, I explained, "In the world I come from, bat dung was good fertilizer. Maybe it's the same here. It's conveniently located right next to the farmland, so we might as well test it."

Cave-dwelling bat dung contained phosphoric acid, making it good, quality manure. I came up with the idea because I knew that in the past, in Southeast Asia, people would extract saltpeter from piles of bat droppings on cave floors to use for gunpowder.

"I have a question for you both: In this world, do people happen to make greatbat dung into gunpowder?"

Mizuho shook her head, but Troach's eyes lit up. "I've heard of that! I've heard the price of animal poop goes way up before wars! Once, someone said they wanted to go poop-raiding, but I turned them down."

"Thought so. Then it should be the same in both worlds—we can use the greatbat dung as fertilizer."

"Huh? Hold on. Wouldn't we get more out of selling it instead of making it into fertilizer? Or we could make our own gunpowder instead."

"We can't do that, Troach. Selling it for money might make sense if we had established trade routes, but our nation can't afford that. We need to secure a stable supply of food first."

"Hmmm. I suppose. But wouldn't it still be good to have gunpowder? We can get resources if we take over nearby parts of the dungeon, but we'll need weapons to do that."

"You're not wrong, but...," Mizuho cut in.

"How much of a scarcity are firearms and bombs in this world?" I asked.

The girls exchanged glances.

"Scarcity?"

"He's asking how common they are," Mizuho quickly clarified.

"Oh. I'd say pretty common. A little expensive, though," answered Troach.

"Yes... You can easily buy them with money. As you might imagine, they see a lot of use."

"In that case, if we need gunpowder, we'll buy it," I decided. "That should be enough."

If it came to it, we could actually extract saltpeter from human and livestock excrement, too. However, we'd need to boil it down or filter it out, which would be an incredibly smelly affair and, speaking bluntly, a troublesome task.

The basic rule of survival was to use whatever you had. Unless you were conducting experiments for personal interest or purposely tackling difficult challenges for likes and upvotes, there was no need to indulge in meddlesome things. If gunpowder was in circulation, we could simply purchase it.

That choice presented a new problem, however. What were we going to buy it *with*?

One morning, after a few busy days of work, the answer would come to us from elsewhere.

24

I woke up at an early hour and left the palace to bathe myself. The brightening starlight was illuminating the Great Fracture. Dawn was always somewhat quiet in Million Dungeon. Footfalls on stone resounded through the morning mist and echoed off the walls.

The river, which flowed down the Fracture to our level, formed a waterfall here before plummeting into the abyss. As I went to the river's edge, I could see several pools dug into the ground, guiding the flow of water. Since it was too dangerous to enter the swiftly coursing stream directly, we'd made canals that were safe for everyday use.

Each of the pools dug along the waterway was about knee-deep; the people bathed and did laundry here, and I was no exception.

Keeping yourself hygienic was a life-and-death matter in survival situations—and not just because the stench could grow unbearable. Uncleanliness led to infection, and it would draw insects that preyed on people. It was a stroke of luck that we'd acquired fire and flowing water at an early stage. Thanks to these, we could cross public hygiene off our list of concerns.

I took off my clothes and got into the cold water, then wiped myself from head to toe with a piece of cloth. I brushed my teeth with a toothbrush I'd made from the crushed ends of small branches, rinsed my mouth, then washed my underclothing and socks and wrung them out. We had all suffered through the disaster with only the clothes on our backs, so the lack of spare garments was a shared challenge. Our kingdom did have a few seamsters who'd fashioned sets of underwear from scraps of cloth. Sadly, our demand outweighed the supply. As such, we'd formed a new custom: We would wash our underclothing and put it back on while it was still wet, then go straight to the campfires and dry off while putting on the rest of our clothing.

At some point, people had established another blaze near the waterway and made a changing-room-slash-laundry-hut with male and female sections. It hadn't been there the previous day. I looked it over with keen interest as I washed my socks.

Meaning to put some wood into the fire to dry my underclothing, I got out of the water and headed for the hut.

It was then that I noticed the very large object just past the makeshift laundry room. Astonished, I dropped into a ready pose as the thing slid out from behind the structure.

It…looked like a goldfish. An enormous goldfish.

That was no exaggeration. It was an actual goldfish floating in midair, with a saddle on its back and reins attached to a mouthpiece. It looked at me with eyeballs that were about the height of my own head, then glanced away, uninterested.

Snapping out of it, I peered into the hut. As I'd thought, someone was there, sleeping next to the campfire.

"Hey," I called to him.

The man gave a start and looked up. He had a squarish face, eyes like saucers, and pointed ears. Before I could ask who he was, he widened his eyes, and he said:

"Eh? Is that a barbarian I see?"

"What?"

I only noticed from following the man's gaze that I was still stark naked. As I donned my wrung-out underclothing and shirt, feeling like an idiot, the man watched me very suspiciously.

"…'Scuse me. Who are you? What are you doing?"

"Oh? The barbarian can speak, it seems." The man twisted his big mouth into a smirk as he sat himself upright. "I am a traveling merchant. I passed by here late last night, but you were all asleep. So I borrowed a fire, content to wait until morning. I had no idea this was a nation of *barbarians*."

"I see. Sorry for not having anyone to welcome you after coming all this way. But I do have a piece of unfortunate news for you. This place you stayed the night in—it's our nation's changing room for women."

"Oh, bless my soul!"

"Such an extreme case of indecency warrants a grave crime in this nation, sir merchant."

"And to whom do I have the pleasure of speaking, sir barbarian?"

"Me? Well, I suppose I'm *in charge* of this nation, for the moment."

"For the moment?" The broker looked at me dubiously before comprehending, and he clapped his hands together. "I see, I see. I had entertained the possibility since first glance. You have a regal presence. It is my utmost honor to make your acquaintance. Please allow me to be fair and just, equally and mutually beneficial. Would you be interested in business dealings, sir rustic-and-in-charge?"

The man introduced himself as Latten of the Five Stars. He took a seat on the piece of wood marking the entrance to the palace, then unfurled a rug with practiced movements and lined up one item after the next, all having come from the goldfish's saddlebag. (Apparently, the creature was called just what it looked like—a goldfish. In Million Dungeon, there was a creature called a crossing-fish that flew in the air, and goldfish were a domesticated type of those.)

Having arisen by now, the citizens livened up at the merchant's visit and were practically falling over one another to get a good look. Of course, they were all disaster victims and didn't have much on them, but Latten agreed to barter and dealt with the many customers one at a time.

The commotion ended about two hours later. Everyone left in groups of two or three, after which Latten put some tobacco in a long, slender pipe and took a puff of it.

"Looks like you did some good business," I remarked.

"You are gracious to let me borrow the front of your dwelling, Your Majesty."

"You're welcome—though I'm not the King. I'm Taiga."

"And your title is...?"

"Taiga the Special," Mizuho cut in from behind before I could answer.

Latten swiveled his gaze over in her direction. "I have never heard that name before."

"I'm new around these parts."

Looking in turn at Mizuho, who was waiting behind me, and then Troach, who was leaning against a pillar, Latten grinned. "Let us then leave smaller dealings aside and move to larger matters."

"Larger matters?" I repeated.

"My primary work is trading with nations. I buy up what you possess too much of and provide that which you need. Foreign trade, as it is known."

"It doesn't look like you came with that many things."

Latten rolled his eyes in exasperation. "I deal with entire nations, so I require preparation. What I have with me is not everything. Once we establish a deal, I will come with the main group. Tell me, what do you seek?"

Troach glanced at me. She probably wanted to ask if she should bring out the jewelry she was hanging on to. Using my eyes, I instructed her to wait.

"If there's a deal to be made, the first things we'd want would be medical supplies."

Latten nodded deeply. "Naturally. New nations always want to explore the labyrinth and expand their territory despite the dangers—and everyone is short on medicine. Very well. I can provide most remedies. Potions to heal wounds immediately, all-purpose medicine chests with everything you need already included, and even love draughts to pierce the heart of the one you have your eyes on."

"We also require clothing. We were caught in the recent dungeonstorm, so we have a fundamental need for daily necessities."

"I've heard about it from some of the customers. What a terrible storm that was. I took major losses myself—two of my warehouses were washed away outright, and several client nations vanished. Still, I have that to thank for being able to make new partners like this. Anything else? If you're going into the dungeon, would you happen to need weapons and armor?"

"Let's see… Any good blades would be nice. And if you deal in weapons that use gunpowder, I'd love to see what you have."

"Yes, yes. I have a good idea now. In that case, please tell me what it is you can sell me."

"Well, unfortunately, we have nothing to sell."

Latten raised an eyebrow and regarded me with suspicion.

"I'm serious," I stated. "As you know, our nation was created from the survivors of that dungeonstorm. There are many things we require, but nothing we can offer."

"And? Just so you're aware, credit won't work. Business in Million Dungeon should be treasured, for it may never recur."

"I'm sure. So I'm asking you to sell it for free. In exchange, I'll work for you."

Latten burst out laughing. "My, you are a cheeky one! And what is it *you* can do?"

"I'm a soldier. One with a lot of training, so I should be able to help. I'd like you to find me an employer who pays well. If you do, half of my payments will go to you."

Latten raised his other eyebrow. "You—a Landmaker—would sell yourself for mercenary work?"

"Basically, yeah."

"Taiga?!"

"Taiga, you can't do that!"

Mizuho and Troach both gave surprised objections.

Latten scrutinized me for a short while as if trying to judge whether I was serious, but eventually, he grinned and shook his head. "Well, that is an interesting proposition. Unfortunately, I must refuse. I cannot afford to do introductions for someone I don't even know."

I could hear Mizuho and Troach breathe sighs of relief.

"I see...," I said. "But in that case, we really *don't* have anything to sell."

Latten looked hard at me and chuckled to himself. "Taiga the Special, was it? I think I understand why you have that title. I've traded with hundreds of Landmakers before. I don't see your type very often."

"Is that so?"

"Now, don't get too down. I was perfectly aware that a poor, new nation like this would have nothing to offer. You know, you would be quite surprised how many things others possess that they believe is worthless."

Latten took a look around the palace. People were busy working in various spots. It was a communal space, a palace only in name. Looking back to me, he said, "One choice you have if you don't have any excess production is to sell people. Not as slaves, mind you. When a nation's population grows too big for its territory, they give some citizens to those who don't have enough. As far as I can see, though, you don't have enough people to be able to auction anyone."

"Any less than this, and our nation won't be able to function," Mizuho cut in.

"Indeed. Your next option is to sell land. Not every room you take control of while exploring the labyrinth will be usable. This goes hand in hand with population, too. People get ahead of themselves and build facilities that end up going unused all the time. I can purchase things like that as well, but..."

"We started with only this palace, so we can't afford to lose what scant territory we possess," Troach commented.

"I figured as much. Which means there is only one thing remaining you can trade—and that is *information*."

"Information..."

"Even rumors have worth in this world, where every place is isolated. Legends, stories of the past, maps, magic research materials... A simple book could get you food for a few days. So? What do you think? Have any news you believe valuable?"

Troach and I both turned to Mizuho. She widened her eyes, but then she snapped out of it and said, "Yes! I'm a storyteller! One with a very long lineage, too, so I have plenty of tales and legends!"

Latten twisted his mouth into a grin. "See? Everyone underestimates the worth of what they have. The trick in business is to carefully dig up what that is." Tapping his pipe to get rid of the tobacco leaf and putting in a new one, he continued. "Let us begin the negotiations."

Talks proceeded, with lunch in between. (Greatbat and boiled bloodsucking kudzu sprouts were the only things on the menu.) Mizuho would briefly mention things she knew as they came to mind, and Latten would set a price for the information as a whole. Along the way, he would propose items we could purchase for that price, and we told him what we wanted.

About three hours passed before talks wrapped up. Thankfully, in addition to securing several kinds of resources, we were able to buy some of the weapons and armor Latten had brought with him as immediate trades.

Latten rolled up his rug, stood up, and stretched his back, seeming satisfied. "Phew! Splendid, splendid. I do love good business. The next time I come, it will be with the goods, so tell me the rest of the information I purchased at that time. And don't sell it to any other merchants before that, please!"

After seeing off Latten, Troach came up to me and asked quietly, "Hey, Taiga, why didn't we sell any of the gold?"

"We probably wouldn't have been able to buy much with it."

"I suppose not, but still..."

"More importantly, what was that all about?!" demanded Mizuho angrily, pressuring me. "Leaving us to make money? This isn't a joke! Don't you understand how much everyone depends on you, Taiga?! Leaving alone to work... It's..."

"I understand that, but I thought it would be quickest if I were to sell my skills—"

"No! Never say anything like that again. If you're going to insist you're not our King, then as Minister, I forbid it. I hereby forbid any Landmaker from leaving the Great Camp Bravo Kingdom without permission!"

Finished, Mizuho spun around and walked away, her boots clicking on the floor.

"Now she's mad...," I murmured.

Troach said, "Look, I get it. In general, I think more like you do than she does. But...do you remember the song called 'Red Rain of Bells' that Mizuho brought up to the merchant?"

"I recall the title. He didn't buy it, saying it was one everyone knew, but..."

"It's about a man who leaves his wife to go on a journey. When he returns, there's an extra wall that wasn't there before, and he weeps now that he's separated from his kingdom for life. Little changes often happen due to dungeoncore shifts. I don't know how things were back in your world, but in Million Dungeon, not being able to see someone again after parting happens all the time. Plus, Mizuho was just forever separated from a lot of her acquaintances herself. You may not have meant it like that, but I think she took it differently."

"...I see."

"This is just my guess; I'm not Mizuho. Still, I don't want you to leave again, either, Taiga. You're unlike any man I've ever met before, and without you, things would be boring," Troach stated, scratching her neck. "I'm gonna go check on her. See you later."

She went off to follow Mizuho, leaving me behind alone. My eyes were on Latten as he loaded his things back into the goldfish's saddlebag. I left the palace and walked over to him.

After turning around, the merchant asked, "Forget to buy something?"

"It's a personal request, but... Do you deal in tea? I'd like some tea leaves."

"I get a lot of orders for tobacco and alcohol, but not tea. How much would you like?"

After asking several people, it turned out tea leaves were not commonplace in this world. As far as drinks went, booze was far more well-loved. Funnily enough, coffee existed as a luxury item, but they said it was no drink for commoners. Roasted wheat and beans, as well as boiled-down nuts and fruits, were on the markets as "tea," but actual teas weren't very popular, possibly given the high price of the leaves.

"Tea leaves dampen quickly, so I don't normally deal in them. But if I get any, I'll bring them to you."

"Thanks for that."

Latten brought the goldfish so low that it was almost touching the ground, then climbed up onto the saddle.

"Come to think of it," I began, "how did you get here? Traveled through the dungeon?"

"No, no. I followed the Great Fracture here. You've built a nation in a good place. Really stands out both from above and from the other side."

That was when it first hit me. Latten was riding a flying mount. Thus, he could travel between the two sides of the Great Fracture. He freely could move up and down the steep cliffsides as well.

Which meant you could easily attack this nation from across the Fracture using the same means of transportation... I'd thought having our settlement against the cliffside would make it defensible, but the truth couldn't have been more different.

"My, that is a severe look," the merchant remarked.

"Sorry... It just doesn't seem like an excellent location to me."

"Hmm? Oh—you're worried about being invaded? You'll be fine. Most people would be too scared to cross such a wide-open area. The divide is so large that it might actually go up to the heavenfloors and down to the deepfloors. Landmakers aside, ordinary people would probably soil themselves at the prospect. I actually passed by several kingdoms as I traveled along the Fracture to reach you, but most of them built walls on the side of the canyon to block out the chasm for fear of large areas."

Latten pointed to the other side of the Great Fracture.

"Right across from here, two floors up, there's another nation. Though I visited it, they didn't talk to me. I'm not sure why they were so cautious, but they fired a large crossbow at me. From the looks of it, they weren't affected too heavily by the dungeonstorm. Still, something must be wrong."

"Didn't crossing the gap make you nervous?" I asked.

Latten offered an intrepid grin. "Of course. But I couldn't pass up a chance like this. The sweetest places to do business are the ones where fellow merchants won't go."

Latten swung the reins, and his goldfish rose without a sound, its fins fluttering as it turned its rear end to me.

"Honestly, don't worry yourself over it. The only ones who would ever travel along this cliff are merchants like me, who simply do not care, and reckless daredevil heroes. A polite reception is never a bad choice when dealing with either. See you again!"

Swinging its tail fin, the goldfish left, crossing the river and turning out of sight around a bend in the gorge.

I returned to the palace feeling anxious. The nation on the opposite cliff face concerned me, but I'd belatedly realized that the Great Fracture itself was a complete and utter security concern. Million Dungeon was apparently no stranger to invasions and wars.

Despite what Latten said, we couldn't afford to leave the matter be, either. The people of our country were proof enough of that. Initially, the Great Fracture induced vertigo and nausea in them. However, after only a few days, they'd grown so accustomed to it that heading to the river and bathing was no problem. This was partly out of necessity, but if *they* overcame their agoraphobic tendencies, others would, too, in time.

Humans weren't the only threat, either. I had to assume there were monsters capable of flying across the gap, like Latten's goldfish, or crawling along the cliff walls. We were utterly defenseless as it was.

And that was how I ended up worrying myself sick over how we'd deal with an attack from the Great Fracture.

Contrary to my expectations, however, our first invader came from *inside* the dungeon.

25

It was the third evening after Latten's visit.

With the starlight having dimmed, and as the people were finishing their work and making preparations for nightfall, there came a commotion from the passage north of the palace as a man with disheveled hair ran to us.

"Help me! We're under attack!!" he shouted, coughing up blood. He fell, and everyone gathered around to support him.

At the time, the three of us had been discussing plans to defend the side of our kingdom that faced the Great Fracture, but we'd run to the gathering crowd after hearing the noise. The man turned to me and spoke, breathing shallow.

"Ogres. The fields are being attacked. If we don't act soon, they'll eat everyone..."

Leaving us with only that, the man passed out.

"Ogres?"

"Ogrekin—the mortal enemy of humankind," Mizuho stated, face stern. "I had thought we would run into them sooner or later. Let's hurry."

We armed ourselves and ran into the northern passage. As we neared the end of the greatbat cave, which was illuminated by a few torches, we spotted them. A group of creatures the likes of which I'd never seen before was jogging after the fleeing townspeople.

They were about one meter tall—half that of an adult human, but quite a bit wider and stockier. Their bodies looked too large for them, they were covered in short brown hair, and they had stubby arms and legs. Their heads were as wide as their bodies, and a big ear hung off either side. Each pair of large, front-facing eyes was glaring. The things resembled short-haired dogs walking on their hind legs. All of them had belts around their waists, with red scarves covering their mouths. Their armaments were shabby, broken swords, rough clubs, rusted hammers, and the like. One of them was clearly using a potlid as a shield.

"Ogrelings, Taiga," Troach explained. "They're weak, but annoying in numbers," she continued. "Make sure you don't get surrounded."

"Understood."

Seeing us armed, the band of ogrelings stopped, appearing frightened. In the meantime, the fleeing citizens hid themselves behind us.

"Situation?" I asked.

"While we were setting up the farms, they suddenly... They came out of the hole in the hill!"

"They got three of us. I don't know if they're dead. At least one was captured..."

As I listened, the enemy forces, which seemed to have collected themselves, readied their weapons and inched closer. There were five in all.

Troach was the first to move. Her thrown dagger plunged deep into one of the ogreling's heads, sending it crashing to the floor. As the other ogrelings charged, I met them with my spear. Their movements were untrained, and dealing with them was easy. Even Mizuho was able to take one down with her own weapon. Troach and I handled the last two, which were flailing their equipment about wildly. The battle was over in a matter of seconds.

We hurried on ahead. When we came to the pitfall in the middle of the passage, we hesitated a bit.

Our intent had been to bury the trap so it was safe. We'd modified the switches, thrown open the cover, and placed a board across it by the wall to allow workers to move through. But now, peering into the hole, we saw a large number of ogrelings had fallen into it and died.

Troach, Mizuho, and I crossed the planks and proceeded through the passage. The treant-hill room was different since the last time I'd seen it.

The star I'd picked up in the slime chamber was hanging in a high spot from the ceiling. It was evening now, so it had dimmed quite a bit, but there was still enough light to barely make out what was happening.

The treant's corpse had been cleaned up by scavengers and our citizens' axes. As for the moss originally growing here, we'd gathered it all up to expose the soil on the floor. We were in the middle of turning the room into a usable plot of farmland, and about half the chamber was ridged now, having been plowed. Several ogrelings were dead by the walls. It looked like some of the remaining bloodsucking kudzu vines were coiled around them. The monsters seemed to die pretty easily.

However, a group of those weak creatures was currently trying to kidnap some of our nation's people. They were clustered around the top of the hill, shouting to one another as they tried to drag the humans they'd caught with their nets into the hole.

I approached them with a shout, and the ogrelings turned to me and charged down the hill. Some of them went too fast and tripped over themselves. They never got back up. Troach caught up and came alongside me, making it the two of us against the oncoming crowd of ogrelings.

Even professional martial artists renowned as invincible in the ring were occasionally killed by nobodies on the street with knives. Blades were powerful things, and facing down so many monsters at once was frightening. Troach and I had spears, which gave us the advantage of range, but the ogrelings kept on running at us fearlessly even though they were about to die. They would be no joke if this devolved into a melee. As we were desperately stabbing, batting aside, and pushing away the enemy, both of us ended up sustaining several wounds.

Meanwhile, Mizuho went around behind and cut the captives out of their nets. They were bleeding as well, but they crawled down the hill under Mizuho's protection and escaped.

That was when we heard a cracked gong from inside the pit. When the ogrelings heard it, they stopped. When it struck several more times, the remaining monsters began to withdraw—growling in intimidation at us all the while—and returned into the hole, one after the next.

Once the last ogreling was gone, the thrumming stopped. Our surroundings suddenly quieted, and under the quickly dimming star, only heaps of ogreling corpses lay upon the disturbed ridges.

Troach and I ran over to the three people Mizuho had rescued.

"Everyone alive?"

"Yes, but they've been beaten severely. They need healing, and quickly."

"Troach, can you move? We need help. Bring a bunch of people here."

"Got it!"

Troach swiveled around and ran back. Mizuho got to work, stopping the blood with what tools she had on hand. Before helping her, I had one more task.

"Mizuho, I'm going to check to see that our foes have actually retreated. Can you handle things here?"

"Huh…?"

"We need to make sure it's safe. I'll be back in a moment," I told the obviously uneasy Mizuho before peering into the pit. A crude ladder was hanging from it. I put a lantern on the tip of my spear and stuck it inside to light the way below. There were no enemies as far as I could see.

Closing the lantern's shutter, I removed the firefly star from within and put a foot on the ladder. Descending several rungs, I looked around, then threw the star I'd taken into the room, as far from the shaft as I could get it. It was nothing compared to a flash-bang, but it would at least be a distraction.

As I listened to the sound of the luminous stone bouncing away, I kicked off my perch and jumped down the remaining distance myself. Using my whole body to soften the impact, I stayed low, quickly scanning the chamber's interior.

It was empty. The firefly star shone quietly in a corner of the room.

Standing, I retrieved my light source and returned it to the lantern, closing the shutter. I approached the open doorway, peeking inside while keeping myself concealed, and saw several flames flickering deeper in the giant hall. The ogreling band was beating a retreat, torches in hand. The dust that had gathered on the floor now had many footprints in it.

Suddenly, I heard the gong ring out a few more times, and the opposite side of the tunnel brightened. Many more torches were visible compared with just moments ago. Perhaps they'd come out a different door. I watched closely, squinting to discern the figures in the flickering orange light. Several larger forms bickered about something in bestial voices as they milled about the little ogrelings. Many of them stood taller than humans, and one was absolutely giant. By my judgment, it had to be over six meters high.

The force of ogrelings we'd fought had only been a reconnaissance group. This was a raid force composed of dozens of monsters.

26

After returning to our land and patching up the wounded, I used some chunks of charcoal to draw the enemies I'd scouted on the wall. I would have liked a camera, but for now, I'd just have to make do with my artistic re-creations.

"As far as I could confirm, there were about forty ogrekin. One of them seemed like the leader. Additionally, there were three enemies with relatively well-built bodies that were taller than humans. It was too dark to make out their features, but their silhouettes implied they each either had horns or were wearing hats or caps."

The eyes of those crowding around were glued to me as I continued my report.

"There was also...one humanoid monster four times the size of a person. I thought it was a statue at first, but it was definitely moving. That far side of the hall was spacious and dark, with the only light coming from the torches. I admit I could have missed something, but those were all the hostiles I saw. It's not much, but can anyone make heads or tails of this?" I asked.

Mizuho was the first to speak up, inquiring, "What did the ogrekin's leader look like?"

"A little skinny, with facial hair. And it looked older. It had several decorations on the ragged clothes it wore."

"That would be a shaman. They can be trouble; they instigate the ogrelings. I believe the horned ogres you saw were a type called beast ogrekin."

"What about the biggest one?"

"Most likely...that was an ogre giant. A terrifying creature that will even eat friendly ogrelings if they're in reach."

A frightened stir rippled through the dark of the palace.

All ogrekin ate people. That simple fact was more than enough to express how threatening they were. Everyone agreed that even those stupid-faced ogrelings couldn't be taken lightly.

I turned back toward the northern passage. After retreating from the farmland with the wounded, we'd put out all the torches in the great-bat cave and blocked off the route with a barricade made of as many things as we could pile up. We also hung spoons and forks from strings to act as alarms, but those countermeasures were all we could manage in such a short time frame.

What would we do if the ogres attacked now? Everyone would be eaten. Most folk's expressions made it plain that they had already given up. If I let them be, they'd panic.

How do I keep them calm?

Immediately, I took the flashlight from my waist and flicked it on. There was a chorus of startled cries as everyone covered their faces. I hadn't turned on my SureFire in quite a while, so it dazzled me as well.

"Everyone, please calm down. We're going to be all right." After confirming that I'd snuffed out the fires of panic, I turned the flashlight off. As everyone blinked, I continued, "It's not over yet. Enemies will be at our doorstep before long, but I know you all—and I trust we can handle it."

"He's right. You're all getting a little too worked up," Mizuho added right away, raising her voice. "We survived that storm, didn't we? And our nation has Taiga. The incredible soldier of the Regiment, come from another world—Taiga the Special!"

"Yeah, yeah!" Troach cheered as though she were an unrelated bystander.

Mizuho took it in stride and carried on. "We have to believe in the one who's saved us countless times, often endangering himself to do so. Taiga will think of a way to defeat this threat. You can be sure of it. Isn't that right, Taiga?"

"Uh... Yeah. I promise to give it my best."

"See? Did you hear that, everyone? Three cheers for Taiga! Three cheers for the Great Camp Bravo Kingdom!"

With Mizuho and Troach stoking everyone's enthusiasm, the people raised their voices. I groaned to myself. That was one more Colonel Kurtz point for me.

After all the praising, Mizuho raised a hand. "The three of us will now hold a war council. Please make sure you know your watch shift, and if you don't have anything to do, then get some rest. Until then, await further instructions! Dismissed!"

We'd avoided a general panic, at least. Still, no one looked especially hopeful.

"Thanks for that," I whispered to Mizuho.

"You're welcome... What will we do?"

"I've been thinking about it. Even with all the tricks in the book, I'm not sure we can drive off a raiding party of that size. And even if we did, we'd probably have to abandon both our new locations."

"A difficult situation indeed."

If the enemy invaded our nation's territory via the farmland and went through the cave to attack the palace, the two passages connecting the three areas would be choke points. Both of them were sturdy stonework partway through, but if we could get one to collapse, we would be safe.

Unfortunately, that was only true if I assumed that these ogres were capable of what humans were. That ogre giant, or whatever that had been, wouldn't be able to go through human-sized doorways or the farmland shaft, but with its sheer size, I'd be better off treating it like an armored vehicle that could crash through most obstacles. The battle with the treant had taught me how dreadful Million Dungeon's monsters were. The tree had restricted movement, though. It was unwise to assume every big monster was just as slow.

I'd heard something shocking while carrying the wounded back here. The ogrelings were tied with humans for the title of weakest race in Million Dungeon. In other words, normal humans were no better than ogrelings. Pretty much all the monsters inhabiting this world were stronger than us.

It wasn't actually that different from how weak humans were on Earth, either. A house cat could best its owner if it went all out. Over there, most creatures would avoid combat; pets didn't need to compete for food. Here, though, things were different. As the weakest race, the only way to survive was to band together, create a nation, and protect ourselves against the labyrinth's threats. I was finally starting to realize why Landmakers were so revered.

Troach pointed to my flashlight. "That lantern really is bright. You say it's not a star? Even searchlight stars aren't usually that strong."

"I thought the same," Mizuho said. "It seems like it would make a powerful weapon against the enemy. Why not?"

"Well…" I pointed the flashlight on the floor and flicked the switch on and off a few times. "It could probably give them pause for a short time, at least. Against one, it could be the deciding factor. But it isn't going to do anything against that group."

The monsters had been using torches, and they *had* ventured into illuminated areas, albeit during the evening. They were nothing like those animals who were afraid of flames or light.

On top of that, the flashlight had recently started flickering oddly. It was probably because of everything it had gone through since arriving in Million Dungeon and because its battery was getting low. I couldn't afford to rely on it and have it go out.

I was painfully aware of our need for military power. In Million Dungeon, fighting had to happen in groups in narrow rooms and passages. Without bolstering our troop power by equipping our people with weapons and armor, they'd run over us with the force of their numbers.

When is Latten returning?

If we sealed off the passages and waited for the merchant to bring in his goods, we could expand our armory. Even then, Troach and I were the only ones who could really fight on the front lines, which would be very difficult. Troach's fighting style was a hit-and-run outboxing style, and my tactics were similar. I was on the scrawnier side in the Regiment. And the simple prospect of a one-versus-many close-quarters combat situation put us at a tactical disadvantage.

Was there no choice but to abandon the farmland and endure?

While I was lost in contemplation, the citizen currently standing watch outside the palace at the Great Fracture suddenly shouted, "Someone's on the cliff—they're coming this way!"

Troach, Mizuho, and I exchanged stupefied glances. Had the attack from the Great Fracture arrived?

When it rains, it pours…, I thought grimly.

I ran over, the other two following. We sprinted past the confusion of the palace and outside.

"Taiga, over there!"

The lookout (it was Lostobi the Death-Cheater) pointed to a light coming this way from the Great Fracture. The silhouette climbing the cliff face was clearly not human...

What is that? An enormous insect? A spider?

It was scaling the sheer face at a shocking speed. As I readied myself, I wondered what the monster was this time. It turns out it was a six-legged lizard. Keeping balance with a long neck and tail, it dexterously moved up the almost-vertical cliff and landed in front of the palace.

The reptile had a saddle on its back, and a person in armor was gripping the reins. They barked a quick order, and their mount stopped immediately. The light had been from the lantern attached to the saddle.

The rider removed their helmet and shook their head, revealing wavy blond hair that caught the light thrown off the bonfire—a woman. A stunningly beautiful one, in fact, with green, glittering eyes and a shapely nose. She gave a comfortable smile and stated, "Hello, good people! Good evening!"

"...Who are you?" I asked.

She put a hand to her breastplate. "I am Astoria the Wing-Blessed, a traveling knight. I couldn't help but notice your bonfires, so I stopped by. If you wouldn't mind, my good sir, I seek lodging for the night."

"A knight..."

I gave her another look-over. Her gear was well-worn, with little cuts and dents all over. The reptile she was riding had armor in some places as well, but that was equally battered. Even the scales covering its body had several blade wounds and claw marks on them, showing that it had been through the same fierce combat its rider had.

"The only ones who would ever travel along this cliff are merchants like me, who simply do not care, and reckless daredevil heroes," Latten had said.

"Forgive my rudeness in asking, but... Are you, well, strong?"

The knight named Astoria tilted her head back and gave a hearty laugh. "Indeed I am, good sir! I was but a wee three years of age when I lopped off the head of my first ogreling. Ever since then, I have fought in battle after battle, braving danger after danger, never leaving three days in between. Million Dungeon may be large, but not three people in it can resist three strikes of my blade!"

I could see Latten's smirk in the back of my mind.

"A polite reception is never a bad choice when dealing with either." The rest of his advice echoed in my mind.

I chose my next words carefully. "Welcome, Astoria the Wing-Blessed. I am a Landmaker of this Great Camp Bravo Kingdom, Taiga the Special."

"Sir Taiga, is it? A pleasure to make your acquaintance."

"If it's fine with you, would you stay in our nation for a time? We're currently in a bit of a dangerous situation, and—"

That was all Astoria needed to hear before her eyes went wide. "Why, of course! I, Astoria, am on a journey in search of adventure. It is an honor—nay, a *privilege* to aid small nations in their times of need. Sir Taiga the Special, I shall gladly accept your kingdom's invitation!"

27

Astoria's reptilian mount was called a horse-lizard, a creature pervasive in this world. As they were wild animals by nature, they possessed hotheaded temperaments, but their willingness to charge at enemies without fear meant many larger nations kept a force of horse-lizard riders. (Judging by Mizuho's explanation, nothing like Earth horses existed in Million Dungeon.)

Astoria's was called Snorts. As the name implied (?), it breathed hard through its nose. The plate that protected its front was riddled with dents and cuts, which one might have assumed indicated a violent disposition. Yet even surrounded by people who weren't its owner, the creature remained calm and didn't make a fuss.

After Astoria had hitched Snorts outside and entered the palace, she was met with wide-eyed stares. Her way of walking with her helmet under one arm exuded confidence, and she never came off as thinking she was better than anyone else. As she cast her glowing gaze all about, she would smile as soon as her eyes met another's. I could easily see that she was quickly captivating both men and women.

"This nation was founded recently, was it not, Sir Taiga?"

"That's right. I'm sorry to say this after inviting you, but I doubt we can provide much in the way of hospitality—"

"Please think nothing of it! I was the one who barged in uninvited after the starlight had dimmed. I am grateful just for being given temporary lodging."

The vivaciousness radiating from Astoria seemed to be swiftly cheering up the citizens. One after another, those whose faces had been dark joined us as we crossed the palace.

With more light on her armor, I noticed that it was not only covered in nicks and dings, but also in sticker-like decorations with letters and symbols written on them. Many were torn or worn away, with new ones placed on top. I made out a few: *Cogwheel Seal of Trust and Interest*, *Looking for New Students for Darkness Mystery Academy*, *Castor Oil Proven to Heal Dungeonblight*, *Friend to Landmakers: The Weekly Hourglass!...*

"What are those on your armor?"

"Oh, these? They're advertisements. I've made a name for myself all over, so folk provide me with activity funds—everyone wins."

I see, I thought. *It must be like motorsport athletes having corporate logos on their uniforms.* Without any television or Internet in this world, though, I'd have thought most information would travel by word of mouth...

We returned to the wall where Troach, Mizuho, and I had been conducting our war meeting, then explained the situation again for Astoria's sake. Not only did she listen fervently, but she would also occasionally ask an incisive question. She pressed me for details on the enemy's armaments, the surroundings' layout, and how many troops our nation could currently muster. The amount of information written on the wall quickly multiplied.

I was impressed in no small measure. Truthfully, I'd predicted a knight would be formal, prideful, and generally difficult to handle, but it seemed I was wrong. She was a proper warrior, one with a good head on her shoulders.

Once the briefing was over, Astoria folded her arms, finally seeming convinced. "I think I understand the situation. Yes indeed. Things look grim for your country. With such a dearth of weapons and troop power, any stratagems we might devise would only delay its destruction."

"Exactly. The only chance is for me to infiltrate them alone and both assassinate their leader and sabotage them, but—"

"—But though you have an abundance of mission experience when it comes to other humans, you have little to none in fighting those accursed monsters, and thus that option would have a significant chance of failure."

I nodded. Astoria was right. I wouldn't have been this cautious had our enemies been human. However, I had neither the knowledge nor the experience to know how capable these ogres were. Any solo infiltration I attempted was sure to fail. What if they had a creature with night vision, or one that could fly and used throwing weapons? As I was now, if they saw me, the only thing I'd be able to do was flee. I couldn't think about this world's monsters with the same rules I used for people. I deeply understood that after the encounters with the treant and slime.

Next to me, Mizuho, voice anxious, asked, "Ms. Astoria, I can tell you are a valiant knight with considerable skill. Would you lend us your aid? With your sword, there is hope even for our nation. Please fight alongside us against the ogrekin!"

"Gladly! Why, I'd planned on that from the start," Astoria replied without a shred of hesitation. Citizens watching with bated breath all gave a cheer at once.

Mizuho's own expression softened with relief, but I still had concerns.

"Astoria, it pains me to say this, but even though you've given your consent to a proposition *we* brought to *you*, we have almost nothing we can offer in payment. All we have are a few pieces of jewelry. When the trader comes back, we should be able to put together a somewhat better sum of money, but..."

"What? There's no need to worry about that. I was never looking for—" Astoria paused in the middle of her sentence. "Wait, that's no good. Oh, they do get cross with me sometimes. Not receiving proper recompense is a burden on those I help. Still... Well..."

After thinking about it for a few moments, she suddenly looked up, her face practically sparkling.

"I know. Lady Mizuho, I have a proposition..."

"What would that be?"

Lofting a smile that did indeed betray how good she thought the idea was, she said, "Would you make me one of the Landmakers of this kingdom?"

"What?!" Mizuho and Troach both exclaimed. I was surprised, too.

Astoria continued gleefully, "It doesn't seem so strange to me. How many stories have you heard where a traveling adventurer grows attached to a kingdom they were passing through and was then welcomed into its Court?"

"But didn't you just *get* here? Are you sure you want to be a Landmaker for a nation you know nothing about? Wouldn't that be *worse* for your reputation than not accepting a reward?" Troach asked worriedly.

Astoria smiled. "You may not believe it, but I consider myself blessed with a good eye for people. I knew at once you were all trustworthy. Lady Mizuho, Lady Troach, Sir Taiga, clearly none of you are accustomed to this, but you still endeavor to save your charges. And *that* is why they follow you. Am I wrong?"

The last question was directed at the citizens all around us. Many were quick to voice their agreement.

"See? There would be no higher honor than to be accepted into such a nation's Court as a friend. And no Knight would ever extort a reward from fellow Court members. What do you think? A splendid idea, if I do say so myself."

For some reason, Mizuho, Troach, and everyone else was looking at me. I had the feeling they were waiting for some kind of grand speech. I was no better at giving addresses than they were.

Without a choice, I cleared my throat and opened my mouth to speak.

"Astoria... We thank you... We couldn't ask for a better offer. Welcome to the Great Camp Bravo Kingdom. From the bottom of our hearts, we would be happy to count you among our ranks."

The biggest cheer since we'd founded the country rang out. Astoria nodded in satisfaction.

"Thank you. There are two large bottles of wine in my things. One a wheat liquor, the other a strong mushroom wine. Both are excellent items. Why don't we pop them open to celebrate our chance meeting?!"

After that, "naturally," we had a feast. This was the first booze anyone had tasted since the dungeonstorm. Many were understandably excited. The commotion seemed a far cry from a kingdom on the precipice of destruction by ogrekin attack. We had two bottles for thirty people. Fortunately, that was not enough for anyone to get too deeply inebriated. At first, I was worried about a surprise attack, but I disregarded the concern and gulped down some wine. Astoria hadn't been lying about its quality, so I took my time savoring the second cup. With how loud we got, it wouldn't have surprised me to learn the enemy drew near but retreated out of caution upon hearing the ruckus.

I made sure to ask Astoria before we went to sleep—there was no tea in any of her bags.

28

Morning came, and the Great Camp Bravo Kingdom citizens began to squirm and awaken from their huddled sleep by the campfires. I, Troach, Mizuho, and Astoria, newly named the Knight of our kingdom, woke up in that order, murmuring good mornings to one another as we outfitted ourselves.

Breakfast was bacon and thin pancakes fried on the Yukon stove, plus boiled bean soup. Though we still had little, Latten's visit the previous day had improved our country's food situation. Things were looking up.

The palace was filled with tension today. We would be going to war. Not hiding behind our barricades, but taking the initiative and invading the ogrekin home ourselves.

With the addition of a stalwart ally in Astoria, we'd come to the conclusion that this was the best option. We would be taking twelve soldiers, with Lostobi the Death-Cheater as their leader. Each was equipped with helmets, armor, and spears. What little weaponry and armor we'd obtained from Latten was a mishmash, and you could tell at a glance that the "fighters" were as well. Still, we needed a long line of spears to take on all those ogrelings without getting quickly surrounded and wiped out. To eliminate as many causes for unease as possible (that of the soldiers as well as my own), we had everyone do a check test, check test, check test with their gear several times. Undoubtedly, they were sick of it by the end.

After Mizuho, Troach, and I prepared ourselves as well, we met before the palace's northern passages. In terms of our equipment, Mizuho had only a spear, Troach had a spear and a dagger, and I wore a wide-bladed weapon shaped like a billhook at my waist along with the spear I carried. Troach and I, plus two specially chosen subordinates, had painted every exposed part of our face and skin with ashes mixed with mud.

I'd had to force the proposition on them. The others were marveling at us.

It took around half an hour to remove the items we'd piled up to serve as barricades. The defenses hadn't been much, in the end.

The heavy footfalls of armored feet approached. I turned around as Astoria, fully geared up with her helmet under her arm, came riding in on Snorts. We exchanged glances and nodded to each other.

"Now then... Let's be off," I said.

Astoria hesitantly raised a hand. "I'm sorry—would you be able to wait a moment? There's something I need to do before we set out."

She took a square plate with fancy edges out of a pocket in her breast-plate. It looked like a black mirror. Was she going to put on war paint? Or would she use it talk to herself and get pumped up? As I watched in fascination, she exhaled a long breath, reached out with her arms, and held the mirror up in front of her.

And then, suddenly, she started speaking to it in a very informal tone.

"Heya, everyone! Y'all still in good health? It's me—Astoria the Wing-Blessed!"

"...?!?!?!?!?!"

Flabbergasted, I stared fixedly. Without seeming to care about the rest of us looking on, she continued, not missing a beat.

"I know it's been two days since my last stream—sorry! Hmm? My producer isn't here today? That's right! I actually, well... I left him behind. Yes, yes, again. Heh-heh. He's probably out of his mind with rage right now. Wouldn't want to see him at the moment! Anyway, you'll never believe it! I now belong to a kingdom! Ta-daa!"

With that, she pointed the square mirror in her hand at us. Mizuho, Troach, and I made suspicious faces at the mirror.

"Its name is the Great Camp Bravo Kingdom! It's a tiny one, just created recently, but it's a super comfy place to be! I'll have everyone introduce themselves—starting with Lady Mizuho!"

"M-me? I'm Mizuho the Frequent Late-Nighter. Oh, and I'm the Minister."

"...What, you want me now? Uhhh... I'm Troach of the Complicated Past... The Attendant, and... Hey, what is this—?"

"Last up is Sir Taiga!"

"......"

"...Go ahead, Sir Taiga!"

"...I am called Taiga the Special... The Ninja..."

"Thank you all! Those three are my new friends. They're the ones who welcomed me into their Court. What? 'That's all'? Yes! This Court has no King! Unusual, isn't it? With that, let's get season six of *Wandering Knight, Astoria's Great Adventure* under way! Title: 'Astoria the Wing-Blessed Becomes a Landmaker'! I hope you're looking forward to it, everyone! See you all later!"

Astoria touched the edge of the mirror, and its surface went black. She sighed, then gave us a happy smile.

"Thanks for going along with that! The viewers seemed to like it a lot. Maybe I should have warned you beforehand, but I wanted to get everyone's raw reactions on camera. Please forgive me!"

"Astoria, would you explain what you were just doing, *now*?"

"Sure. This is called moving-image streaming," Astoria said casually.

"Moving-image...streaming...," I repeated back to her.

She waggled the mirror in front of us with pride. "This allows whatever it reflects to be seen by people in faraway places. It's Cogwheel's latest technology. They took me on as a trial user in exchange for becoming my sponsor. Apparently, they want to have famous adventurers and Landmakers use them to make a big show out of their activities. My stream is pretty popular, too. Even when I'm traveling alone, fans from distant places will still watch. I'm truly honored by their support."

"...I see."

I took a deep breath, trying to calm myself down. "I don't even know where to start with this... What is this Cogwheel?"

Mizuho answered my question. "It refers to one of the world powers, the Holy Capitalist Republic of Cogwheel. They are strong in scientific fields and create all kinds of mysterious items using technology from the deepfloors. This mirror must be one of them." As the young woman explained, she peered into my face, suspicious. "What's going on, Taiga? You're acting oddly."

"Well... Something similar existed in the world I'm from... It just felt...conspicuously similar."

As soon as the words left my mouth, Mizuho's face lit up. "Wait, wouldn't that mean that streaming culture comes from Visitors?!"

"...Yes?"

"I knew it! Songs and stories make it clear that there's been more than a handful of Visitors. Naturally, they brought with them ideas from their worlds and integrated them into Million Dungeon's own! Until now, I've never had the means to confirm it. I'd given up... But with you here, Taiga, now I know!"

Ah... I see. She really is quite the Visitor maniac. Looks like I went and said something I shouldn't have... I looked up, but my eyes found only the dark ceiling.

"Ms. Astoria! I have a *great deal* of interest in that mirror! How do you perform this 'streaming'?!"

"Ha-ha-ha! There's no need to be impatient, Lady Mizuho. I'm happy you've taken a fascination with it. I shall gladly tell you whatever you wish to know."

"Really?!"

"Yes. And if it's all right with you, Lady Mizuho, we could do a collaboration stream. We'll need to decide on a name..."

I watched helplessly as the two young women abruptly got to be good friends. Troach seemed unsettled; she came up next to me and whispered, "Hey, Taiga, is she saying that if I see my face in that thing, people far away will be able to see it, too?"

"You catch on quick."

"Whaaat...? I don't want that. Great... What should I do? I was just on it before, and I even gave my name..."

"Something wrong with that?"

"Come on, you know my previous occupation," Troach stated sourly, scratching at her neck. "Well, what's done is done, but still... I'll have to be careful I don't ever show up on it again if I can help it."

"I feel the same."

"You do? But nobody here knows you."

"It's an ingrained habit from my world..."

I couldn't help but associate this with the incident that led to me retiring from the Regiment. That nightmare in Ankara, where one photo uploaded to Instagram had ruined everything. This situation was completely different, but still...

"Now then, everyone, let us depart! We shall ride on into the depths of the labyrinth and destroy the ogres' forces!" Astoria declared loudly, smoothly unsheathing the longsword from its place on her back. It indeed was an act befitting a model knight: bold and inspiring to all. It was clear just from the deft way she handled her weapon that she *was* as capable as she presented herself. My own experiences only further confirmed that fact. Astoria was *strong*. There was zero problem with us letting her be the outrider of the Court.

Why, then, was my mood not brightening at all?

Perhaps because I'd been in the Regiment for too long. It was the age of frontline soldiers filming combat on GoPros and uploading the footage to the Internet. Had the world left me behind while I'd been handling secret missions that could never come to light?

Such bouts of unease crossed the back of my mind occasionally. And as I led the party into the dungeon, I had no doubt I did so with a sullen expression.

29

Our army (consisting of sixteen people total) left the country and proceeded down the passage.

When we came to the greatbat cave, Troach, our scout, used a hand signal to stop us from following. An ogreling was dead, jammed between stalactites.

"He must have been their scout," Troach concluded, searching the creature's possessions. "Footprints nearby. I'd guess there were two more. They probably came to check on us but panicked and went back after one of them died."

The enemy had been trying to spy on us, it seemed. However...

...when I looked more closely and observed the ogreling, I couldn't find any external wounds on the body caught in the pair of natural stone spikes sprouting from the cave ceiling.

"What got him?"

"I'd guess getting caught between stalactites."

"They can die from that...?"

"They die real easily. But they multiply like nothing else. Out of nowhere, too."

We'd been able to confirm it was safe, so she sent the signal to the rear group, and we resumed our advance. After passing through the cave, we entered the passage to the west. I was a little worried that the horse-lizard Astoria rode wouldn't be able to get through the narrow hallways, but it could bend its six legs to crawl and keep its height surprisingly low as it moved.

Like a tank that could shift to car height using hydraulic suspension, I thought with keen interest.

The reason horses were nonexistent was becoming more apparent.

Their sprinting capabilities were better suited for the vast plains they lived on. Such talents were useless in Million Dungeon.

I'd been watching our whole party closely, but I was especially worried about the twelve subordinates we'd taken along as soldiers.

Even trained fighters sometimes panicked in combat and broke down crying. We'd tried to pick out the most levelheaded people and what few who had prior battle experience, but the farther we got from our home, the more their unease showed on their faces. These folk weren't to blame, of course. We were dragging regular citizens along with us to war. This would be a considerably difficult mission when I thought about leading them as a combat force and bringing them all back alive.

It was indescribably painful for a fellow soldier you'd gone through long, harsh training with to die. I'd experienced it several times myself. How hard would it be if I let these ordinary people perish?

Mizuho and Troach were no exceptions. They both had pluck, and I trusted them to the extent that they wouldn't become hysterical during battle, but neither of them was anything close to a professional warrior.

Would I be able to remain calm if they died?

In the thick of it, I trusted myself to shut out emotions. Yet the same could not be said for after the battle ended and I returned to our nation. Just imagining it made my heart pound harder.

While I was keeping a careful eye on our party's edgy looks as we marched, Astoria brought Snorts over to me.

"Sir Taiga. Are you in good health?"

"...Yeah. No problems here."

"Then try smiling. An anxious general makes for frightened troops," she stated, a mischievous smirk on her lips.

"...I'm a general now?"

"What else would you be, Sir Taiga? All these people of our nation have acknowledged you as such. That is why they follow you. A gloomy expression is not an acceptable answer to their confidence. All you can do is grin even if you don't wish to, stick out your chest, and walk."

Her instructions felt too careless for my tastes, and they irritated me. "I'm bad at faking smiles. Especially when so many lives are on the line."

"Seems like it!" Astoria replied with a laugh. "Look, Sir Taiga. There's a well-known aphorism in the community: A streamer showing their pain won't get views."

"…Yeah?"

"It means that those who try to entertain others must first try to entertain themselves. Are Landmakers not of the same breed?"

"Uh… Maybe?" I said, confused.

Astoria puffed out her chest. "I know exactly how deeply you feel for the people, Sir Taiga. You may leave this to me. I will not allow our troops to die. I'll show the enemy what for!" she declared confidently before leaving my side.

I breathed a sigh. Perhaps I really *was* the most anxious of all. A commander who worried about the dead before even reaching the combat zone was not a very good one.

Though I was still somewhat unconvinced, Astoria's consideration had gotten across. As she'd advised, I lifted my head up and kept on walking, though I gave up on trying to force a smile.

We came to the pitfall; it was open wide. The corpses of the ogrelings that had fallen in were already no more than skeletons. Million Dungeon's scavenger creatures were fearsome things.

After crossing the planks, I opened my mouth and said, "All troops, prepare for battle!"

Everyone with spears readied them. Troach put a hand on her dagger's hilt to make sure she could draw it smoothly. Mizuho checked on her emergency bandages and medicines. Astoria shut her faceplate and gripped her longsword.

I took over the lead of our force from Troach, and we resumed our advance. We entered the farmland room, careful of any ambushes. Many a footstep had trampled the fields, but no enemies were in the chamber.

We headed for the hill in the center and looked down the shaft. Shining a lantern in, we found that the ladder had been brought down and now lay on the floor of the room below us. Our enemy had taken preventative measures against us.

"I'll go first," Astoria said, giving Snorts a slap on the neck. I watched as it, with her still on its back, plodded right over the opening's edge. The horse-lizard's large body stuck to the shaft wall, and it disappeared quickly down the hole. There was the *clack* of hooked nails meeting stone flooring, and after a few moments, the bottom of the hole lit up. Astoria had lifted the cover off her lantern, a signal that it was safe.

She dismounted, picked the ladder off the floor, and sent it back up the hole. I reached out to grab its upper end, then pulled it up and hung it on the wall.

I shuddered at the usefulness of horse-lizard troops within the dungeon. These creatures could move across walls and ceilings with a rider! Knights capable of three-dimensional movement indoors—a nightmarish idea. I'd need to consider the possibility of encountering enemies that could move in the same way. Horse-lizards couldn't have been the only creatures adapted to suit Million Dungeon's environment.

I went down the ladder after Astoria. Once my feet were on the ground, I headed for the still-open doorway, careful to conceal my steps. I peered into the hall. For the moment, the long corridor seemed empty. Two torches burned on either side of a sizable arch-shaped opening at the far end. They were probably about fifty or sixty meters from here. Roughly ten meters closer was the scaffold the ogreling shaman had been on when I'd first spotted it. That rose two meters off the ground.

Wouldn't an ogreling die if they fell from a scaffold at that height?

I began to hear the echoes of bestial howls and growls, accompanied by the distinct sound of metal on stone. I couldn't pinpoint the location, but they couldn't have been very far from the hall.

After returning to the ladder and sending up the signal, our subordinates nervously descended. I watched with bated breath, but fortunately, nobody missed a rung on their climb.

Troach and Mizuho brought up the rear, putting all sixteen people safely down in the room.

I pointed to myself and Troach, and everyone else nodded. As we'd decided in advance, nobody opened their mouth. The two subordinates with ash-painted faces stood next to Troach and me, waiting for instructions with anxious expressions.

After the booze from last night's feast had run out, we'd moved on to a strategy meeting. That was when I'd explained my plan to everyone.

Troach and I, plus two subordinates, formed the scout group. I placed eight under Astoria's command and designated them the raiding group. Mizuho was assigned two guards to form the support group. The scouts would take the lead, then signal behind when things were safe to have the rest of the force advance. We would act as covertly as possible, and as soon as we were spotted, we'd fight them head-on...

In all honesty, I didn't know how effective it'd be to split things up this way. The first question was whether these people could function as a single unit. It relied on our subordinates' work, though not as much as it relied on Astoria's strength.

I'd made one fatal mistake in Ankara: trusting someone I shouldn't have. Was it really the best idea to leave everyone's lives, and the fate of our nation, to this woman, who was both a renowned knight and a *streamer*?

I looked over at Astoria. Noticing my gaze, she smiled and nodded back with no idea what it was I was thinking.

Mizuho, Troach, and all our subordinates were staring at me in the same way. My mind was made up.

When we began the operation, they *would*, without a doubt, mess up in some fashion. These things never, ever went according to the ideal. Some would be wounded and might even die.

But I was doing this job as part of a team, which meant trusting my comrades with my life. And to the last, they believed in me.

Shit… Fine, then. Let's do this.

Signaling my squad, I stepped into the hall. Dust flicked into the air as we trod on the floor, which was marked with the ogrekin's footprints.

Troach and I took the front side by side. Our two subordinates followed just behind, keeping an eye on our six. We'd told them to tap us on the shoulder to notify us of anything strange happening. I'd made them practice it before setting out, too, but it was stopgap knowledge, so I wasn't sure if it would help.

We proceeded with caution, following the passage's western wall. When we came to an empty doorway, we checked inside. Nothing. The lantern light, kept to its minimum, illuminated a fallen bookshelf and some broken dining ware on the floor. Farther along, we passed two similar entrances. The dust on the floor indicated that nobody had gone through them, so it was safe so far.

Now halfway down the hall, the next door we came upon was metal. I checked the door, gauging whether to have everyone else come up. Yet while I was pressed to the side of the entrance, the thing suddenly flew open from inside. The firelight inside the room showed: a muscle-bound man close to two meters in height with goat horns sticking out of his head.

That goat-head looked down at us, seeming taken aback. We were quicker in shaking off the surprise. I flung out my spear, stabbing the creature's neck from below. The point pierced his fur and stopped when it hit hard flesh. A coughing cry came from his throat, at which point, Troach made her move. Her spear lanced in the dark, sinking deep just below the goat-man's jaw. His mouth spasmed, then fell limp. We knew he'd died because all his body weight suddenly pressed down on our spears.

We peered into the room past the corpse. It was all clear. When we drew our weapons back, the goat-man's body slid to the floor. Our two subordinates were frozen in place, staring at him. I waved a finger in front of them to draw their attention, then instructed the pair to go back and keep an eye on the rear teams.

Giving a gesture to Troach, who was looking smug after having trounced an opponent, we each took one of his legs and dragged the goat-man inside the room.

A stove sat at the other end of the room, a fire burning inside. Furniture had been used for fuel. Haphazardly smashed shelves were piled up against the wall. Once, they might have been antiques, if the remnants of their beautiful craftsmanship were anything to judge by. Greasy metal skewers and bones with meat still on them littered the space around the kiln. Had the monster been cooking and eating some creature? Mizuho had said that ogres ate humans. I put the unpleasant imagery out of my mind.

The stove was solidly built out of piled rocks, and its vent reached up and connected to the ceiling. It left me wondering how smoke exhaust and liquid drainage were typically handled in this world. We had a river right next to our country, and the palace opened right up to the Great Fracture, so I'd never had to consider it before. Waste management couldn't be easy in other places. I'd have to ask about the matter later on.

That was when one of the subordinates keeping watch outside the room's entrance frantically tapped me on the shoulder. I turned around as the door on the opposite side of the hall opened, and a legion of ogrelings came pouring out. They'd been heading to the stairs at the end of the corridor leading to the upper floor, but one of them had spotted us somehow.

The door of the room we were in was wide open, and the firelight inside was leaking into the hall. Seeing that, the line of ogrelings stopped and started debating something. As we held our breaths and watched them from the door, they suddenly began to shriek. Drawing swords and clubs, the monsters charged forward on their short legs.

I didn't know what had tipped them off. All they would have seen was the cracked door. Had it been the scent of blood? Did they sense the presence of humans? Either way, now that our cover was blown, the first stage of our mission was over.

There were nine ogrelings total crossing the hall, making almost dog-like barking noises as they went. The last one took a short horn it kept stowed in a scarf and began loudly playing. It sounded like a vuvuzela as it reverberated. The call immediately threw everything into a commotion.

Giving up on hiding, I exited from the doorway. The ogrelings, now directly faced with an enemy, became even more enraged as they charged at us.

Pinching my fingers and blowing into them, I whistled once. A moment later, a muffled, hissing roar rang from the south end of the hall, from which we'd come. The surprised ogrelings stumbled right in the middle of the hall. I watched as Astoria, astride Snorts, showed herself, stepping in from the doorway to the slime room. Snorts opened its mouth wide, stuck out its pink-and-purple tongue, and shook the loose-hanging skin around its neck. From its maw, another of those intimidating, hissing roars sounded.

The eight soldiers under Astoria's command appeared from behind her as she rode in slowly, unfolding into a line of unmatching spears. Behind them were Mizuho and the two soldiers protecting her. She held something high above her—Astoria's black mirror. It seemed she'd been instructed to record this. Was that really all right? There were essential support duties she needed to perform.

I thought of many reasons this mission could end in failure. It was wholly possible Astoria would mistime an attack if she was preoccupied with the stream. If Mizuho got wrapped up in that, too, a tragic disaster would be inevitable...

No, no, calm down, I told myself. We knew we'd be discovered during recon. Both the raiding group and the support group had deployed as I'd told them during the briefing. Well enough to deserve praise, in fact. But the vital part started now.

Astoria, sitting straight in the saddle, called in a voice that carried well, "Hey, hey! I am the great Astoria the Wing-Blessed! Knight of the

Great Camp Bravo Kingdom and moving-image streamer! I come to conquer you lawless ruffians that have invaded our nation's lands and brought harm to its people!"

Her message had caught the ogrelings' complete attention. They diverted their focus from the scout group and began growling threateningly at the armored people slowly approaching.

"Quake in fear, miserable ogres who would do ill to humanity! If you value your lives, then leave here! But if you wish your heads on the floor, then come with as many as you wish!"

I inched back to try and return inside the stove room and nearly stabbed myself in the back with an ally's spear for the effort. The two scouting subordinates were white-knuckle, gripping their weapons, eyes wide in fear, blocking the doorway.

"Back! Back! Get inside!" I yelled, chasing them into the room before following them myself. "Hide behind the doorway! Don't chance any peeks!"

Pushing them into a safe place (and one where they wouldn't accidentally stab a comrade), I beckoned Troach over and hid next to the entrance.

"Earplugs! Hurry!"

Everyone took out scraps of cloth. Astoria had mentioned in the meeting that she planned to use a bomb. My training had prepared me for blasts in closed spaces, but the same couldn't be said of anyone else.

Before our earplugs would block my instructions from being heard, I stated, "Troach, you and I will charge into the hall as soon as the bomb goes off. Wait for my signal."

"Got it!"

"You two follow us. If you can't, wait here. If any enemies come this way, take them out. If you can't do that, then close the door and protect yourselves."

"U-understood!"

"Great—plug your ears. And keep your mouths open."

After stuffing my own ears, I chanced a glance into the corridor again.

I'd only looked away for a few moments, but the hall was in a terrible state now. Weapon-wielding ogrelings had appeared one after the next to join the enemy group. On my first encounter with this force, I'd estimated their ranks to total forty-four, but now there seemed to be even more.

The raiding group pointed their spears forward, knees weak. Still, our opponents were not fools. Deciding the subordinates looked easier to deal with than Astoria, they spread out in the hope of encircling them.

"Left wing, right wing, forward with me!"

Even through the cloth, I could hear Astoria's shout. What I saw a moment later shocked me. Those soldiers, so afraid, had advanced at Astoria's order. A mere eight spears were pressing back against the horde of ogrelings. I couldn't have done that.

Still, Astoria would only be able to suppress the opposition with her own presence for so long. The ogrelings were alert, and reinforcements streamed up from behind to bolster their ranks. As their numbers grew, so too did their aggressiveness. The enemy halted its retreat and clanged their weapons together, looking like they were about to fall upon us like an avalanche.

Still nothing? When will it start? I fretted as I looked on. From atop her horse-lizard, Astoria remained undaunted.

Two large figures appeared in the hall behind the horde of ogrelings. One was a tall ogrekin with the head of a deer. The other, even more massive than the first, sported a bull's head. The deer gripped a long-handled halberd, and the bull, a double-sided ax. An old ogreling rode on the deer's shoulder. It was the shaman I'd seen before. Waving its staff around, it yelled in a hoarse voice to be put onto the scaffold. The contingent of ogrelings cried out in a feverish craze and, a moment later, rushed us like a dam bursting.

As though she'd waited for this moment, Astoria took something out of her saddlebag and hurled it in front of her.

The spherical object traveled in an arc before falling into the midst of the oncoming horde. Not a second later, it exploded.

In the nick of time, I turned away and hid behind the wall. The bomb was more powerful than I'd anticipated. A gust of air rushed in through the doorway, instantly putting out the flame burning in the stove and dropping the room into darkness.

When I looked back into the hall, it was an entirely different scene. The bomb had mowed down the entire charge. Dead ogrelings lay on the floor. Those closer to ground zero had been vaporized.

In the back of the room, the ogreling shaman, the deer-head, and the goat-head were covering their ears, unable to move. But that went for us as well. Several had let their spears fall out of their hands. They were all presumably wearing earplugs, but earplugs obviously couldn't have buffered the shock wave.

Snorts shook its head and blew air out of its nose, seeming irritated. Only Astoria was happy—she turned around in the saddle and shouted behind her, "Lady Mizuho, did you get that?"

"What?! What did you say?!" Mizuho asked, tugging her earplugs out.

"Did you?! Get that?!"

"Ah, yes! I got the whole thing!"

"Very good! Forward, my troops!"

Astoria removed the longsword from her back and held it aloft.

"Long live the Great Camp Bravo Kingdom!"

"...L-long live the Kingdom!"

A scattering of cheers rang in the corridor. They seemed to be still recovering from the explosion's impact, but as Astoria continued, brandishing her claymore, their voices gradually fell into line.

"For glory!"

"...For glory!"

"For victory!"

"For victory!"

"For the views!"

"For...the????"

"Charge!!"

Shutting her faceplate, Astoria smoothly brought her longsword down in front of her. Snorts took off like an arrow fired from a drawn bow. Its hooked claws scraped the floor and threw off sparks, and Snorts, now one with its knight, charged the enemy lines.

The ogreling shaman jumped up and down on its scaffold and barked something in a hoarse voice, causing ogreling reinforcements to come running into the hall. They flooded in from the stairs against the wall and from the trapdoors in the floor we hadn't noticed until now, blocking off and stopping the soldiers trying to follow Astoria.

The bull-head clopped its hooves and stepped forward. It was a giant, twice the size of a human, with muscles all over its body that looked like they'd burst out of its skin. On its pale skin was a tattoo of a tightly packed maze pattern. Its hefty double-sided ax caught Astoria's longsword head-on, producing a metallic clang like a cracked bell. Its hooves slid across the floor, kicking up dust. With the horse-lizard's charge stopped, the knight and the bull-head began a fierce clash.

Behind the bull-head, the shaman continued dancing. The ogreling horde, which had been wiped out just moments ago, was regaining its numbers. Newly arrived ogrelings, perhaps spurred by the sight of the bull-head squaring off against Astoria, fearlessly pointed their spear tips at the soldiers. The situation was steadily became a melee where enemy and ally were mixed—precisely what I wanted to avoid.

I turned back to my team and said, "All right, let's go. We need to take down that shaman. Troach, back me up. You two, watch our backs. Got it? Good. Charge!"

We burst out of the room and started along the wall toward the back of the enemy formation. The shaman on the scaffold spotted us quickly, however, delivering a command and pointing our way. In response, the deer-head stepped to meet us.

Like the bull-head, the deer-head had a maze etched into its skin. This one wasn't a tattoo. Perhaps its race carried the pattern naturally.

It brandished its long halberd, trying to use its reach to overwhelm us. Closer up, its size surprised me. It wasn't as big as the bull-head, but it still towered over an average human. Including its horns, it was over two meters high. The absolute rule of close combat was never to fight anyone bigger than you. Going head-to-head with this behemoth would be idiotic.

Yet if such an encounter couldn't be avoided, what was the best tactic? The answer was simple: Use every means at your disposal to win.

I sped up my pace to throw our opponent's timing off, then jumped in while it swung its halberd into the air. Sliding between its legs, I rammed my billhook into the soft portion behind one of its knees. With a tendon cut, the limb crumpled, and a scream raged in its throat.

Seeing Troach and our two subordinates trying to join me, I shouted, "Go! Go! Get the shaman!"

Troach widened her eyes, but she nodded. She slipped past the kneeling deer-head. The other two nearly stopped out of fear, but after Troach yelled for them to follow, they hurried along.

The deer-head roared in agony and rage. I'd been waiting for that. Turning, I grabbed the tip of one of its antlers and its jaw, then rotated around, using the momentum to put all my body weight forward. Following the principle of levers, a loud *snap* issued from its neck.

The energy left the deer-head's body, and the halberd, which fell from its hands, clattered to the floor.

Ripping out the billhook from the back of its leg, I turned around as Troach and our two subordinates closed in on the shaman's scaffold. Seeing three ogrelings about to pounce on them, I yelled, "Look! He's dead! Look!!"

When they saw me pulling its head up by an antler, the ogrelings visibly wavered. Some succumbed to fear and deserted the fight. As the shaman wailed in rage, someone grabbed its leg from underneath. It was Troach, clinging to the platform.

The shaman raised a hand, and a dully shining star appeared, hovering over its palm. The thing shot down, leaving a trail behind it, skimming right over Troach's head. The move cast a momentary light on the surroundings, causing Troach to yelp.

"You little…"

She hadn't released the shaman's leg. Panicked, the monster tried to kick Troach off with its free foot. At that instant, the scaffold tilted over. Whether it was because of the extra weight or an aftereffect of the shooting star remained unknown. The platform's construction didn't seem all that sound to begin with. Ropes snapped, planks broke, and the entire thing quickly collapsed and fell.

The dust billowing up in curtains obscured Troach and the shaman, both of them having tumbled down along with the debris. From inside, I saw the flash of a dagger, then again. A few moments later, a hand burst out of the dust, holding the green scarf the shaman had been wearing.

Immediately, the nearby ogrelings descended into chaos and began falling over themselves to flee. The disturbance quickly spread to the front lines. The ogrelings that'd been hurrying out of the dark to join the fight turned tail and beat a retreat.

The bull-head screamed something indistinct but no less wrathful. My intuition understood it to be *Don't run! Fight, or I'll kill you!* Try though it did, the monster was helpless to calm the panic. The ogrelings wove around the bull-head's and the horse-lizard's feet as they made their escape.

Astoria wasn't one to let an opponent's distraction go unpunished. Snorts reared up on its hind legs and tried to use its front and middle pairs of claws to slash down from the bull-head's chest to its gut. The massive creature handily guarded it. No sooner had it done so, however, than a longsword cut down from above. The rough steel blade slammed right between its horns, cleaving its head in half and killing it.

The tide had turned, now that all the enemy leaders were gone. What ogrelings remained scurried off with surprising swiftness. It didn't even feel like ten seconds before every last one of them was gone. The next thing I knew, the only ones in the hall were us and the dead bodies.

"Victory!" Astoria shouted.

The corridor erupted into joyous cries. Both the wounded and those holding broken spears cheered in the thrill of victory.

"Long live the Great Camp Bravo Kingdom! Hurrah!"

"Hurrah! Oh—Mizuho, did you get all that?"

"Yes, yes, I got all of it! Is everyone all right?"

Mizuho came running up from the rear. She still had Astoria's black mirror in her hands. She only had one guard with her now, and that one was nursing several wounds. I then realized Mizuho herself had blood on her.

"Mizuho, are you all right?!"

"I'm fine! This is from patching others up."

The wounded soldiers had been laid down along the wall near the entrance. Mizuho seemed to have been busy, what with the healing and the recording.

"Anyone dead?"

"No, but three are unconscious. We need to get them back home right away—" Mizuho paused as her eyes searched all around. "…Where's Troach?"

Troach had fallen in the debris of the scaffold beside the ogreling shaman she'd taken out. Maybe a fragment of the star that had skimmed past her had hit her, for blood was dripping from her forehead, and her eyelids were shut.

Mizuho went white as a ghost and knelt beside the other girl. "Oh no! Troach, you're alive, right?! Please don't die!"

Troach, eyes still shut, answered, "I can't go on… I think I might die… I'm sorry…"

"Hey! No, stop, don't!"

"…Well, I'm definitely wide-awake, so I don't think I'll die yet, but…"

"Stupid! I'll fix you right up, so hold still!"

Troach squealed as Mizuho, who was far from a professional medical attendant, roughly tended to the wounds.

I collapsed and exhaled.

That was exhausting...

I didn't want to go on any missions like this ever again. Sure, maybe the situation had been urgent, but charging into an enemy base with almost zero information? I couldn't be happy about it just because we'd won in the end. It was a miracle this hadn't ended in disaster.

After having Mizuho return her black mirror, Astoria addressed the object. "And that is that! How did you all enjoy it? Easy win, wasn't it? It really was! I'm actually a little unsatisfied. But look at this place!" Astoria said, spinning the mirror around to capture her surroundings. "Can you see it? It goes above, below, all over! Yes, exactly! This chamber clearly leads to new adventures! To tell you the truth, I love the feeling of cutting it close... Did you know that? I guess you already do. Heh-heh-heh. Yep! Danger makes me feel most alive! This nation is brand-new, and it's in a really tough situation. It looks like I'll be getting plenty more footage in the future, so stick around a while!"

Astoria was in a great mood as she pointed the black mirror to me. "Before I end the stream, I'd like a comment from everyone. Hey, Ninja sitting on the floor! Sir Taiga! What are your thoughts?"

"...I want helicopters."

"Hmm?"

The words all came out of my mouth without thinking. "I want trucks. I want drones. I want assault rifles and bullets. I want flash-bangs and grenades. I want radios. I want night-vision goggles. I want plastic explosives—"

Astoria burst out laughing. "Seems Sir Taiga has many needs! If anyone out there watching has any idea what all those things are, please tell me! Now then, next up is Lady Troach—"

And that was when we heard it: an incredible, ground-shaking groaning.

Everyone froze and looked in the same direction. The groan had come from past the large arch-shaped entranceway at the north of the hall. No matter how you heard it, it could only have been made by a creature far larger than any human.

I stood up and shouted, "Everyone, withdraw! Now! Withdraw!"

The sound continued, now accompanied by heavy footfalls. The closer they got, the more visible a pair of eyes and a mouth, like holes burning red, became in the darkness. It appeared from the direction the ogrelings had fled: a giant humanoid monster of ashen-black. Its head seemed to be an animal's skull with two twisted horns growing out of it. The dark, sunken-in eyes set in its face blazed like coals.

This was the giant I had seen here last time. To think this thing still awaited us...

"So this is an ogre giant...," I murmured.

Mizuho shook her head. "An ogre giant? No. Far from it. This is an aberration that lurks in the deepest, darkest depths of the dungeon... Ruler over shadow and flame..." The blue-haired young woman's voice turned hoarse in fear. "Balgor the flame demon."

He opened his mouth and roared in our direction. Fire outlined the fearsome thing's entire form in crimson. On his back were wings that resembled an owl's, as well as a long tail.

Flame gathered in the demon's right hand, then was compressed into the shape of a white-hot longsword. In his left hand was a long flail-whip.

This wasn't a job for an assault rifle...

What we *really* needed right now were anti-tank missiles or something.

30

"Wretched humans."

The monster could talk—which was an utter shock to me.

"How dare you sully my floor-domain with your disgusting feet. I shall turn every one of you to ash. But rejoice! As a reward for making it this far, I will give you a choice. Will you die by the sword, or by the whip?"

As he pontificated, Balgor walked toward us, his footsteps rumbling.

"Retreat! Run away!"

At my yell, our subordinates all began to flee to the rear of the hall at once. But it wouldn't do any good. Not for all of them. We had wounded who couldn't escape, and we wouldn't get away while carrying the unconscious.

The flame demon chuckled and swung down the whip in his left hand; he must have caught on to our predicament. The whip flew through the air like a living creature, destroying the entranceway to the shaft room, walls and all. The escape route before their eyes now blocked off, our subordinates gave cries of despair.

The flame demon narrowed his eyes, seeming pleased.

"It seems you have no intention of accepting my generous proposal—fools! If you will not choose a single means of death, then I shall kill you slowly and painfully."

I desperately racked my brain, but I couldn't come up with a single effective plan of action. Attack his legs and trip him? Not possible. He was clearly not like the deer-head. The skin covering him was like rock; I doubted the billhooks and spears we carried would get through. I felt like I was standing in front of an armored bulldozer.

Troach was in no state to move, and Mizuho was out of the question.

That left either me or Astoria who would have to do something, but even that...

The moment I saw Astoria out of the corner of my eye, I was stunned. Her...her eyes were sparkling. With her visor flipped up to expose her face, those eyes burned with flame.

This woman... This *knight* was an adrenaline addict. She'd just told me earlier she felt joy being in dangerous, life-and-death situations. And she was probably going to stream this, too!

"...Sir Taiga?"

"What? What are you about to do?"

"Don't stop me. I live for moments like these. I will become their shield, become their sword—"

"You just want to revel in the danger!"

"But who else is there? As a Landmaker, now that the people have entrusted me with their hopes, I have a responsibility to confront hardships. Am I wrong?"

She was so hard to deal with—slinging around ideas of great, just causes for her own convenience.

Astoria handed me the black mirror and smiled. "We're live. Make sure you get this, all right?"

"Astoria!"

She shut her faceplate and gave Snorts a kick in the side. The owner and her mount were much alike. With a single loud exhale, the horse-lizard started off toward the flame demon.

"Bastard child of the accursed demonfloors! I will be your opponent!"

"Oh? I will permit you to give your name."

"My name is Astoria the Wing-Blessed! Wandering Knight and Landmaker of the Great Camp Bravo Kingdom! I ask you, monster, that we fight with our swords!"

"Fine. I will grant your wish."

The words had barely left his mouth when he slammed his longsword into the stone floor. It cut deeply, drawing a line of red-hot molten lava.

Snorts jumped right before it cut the horse-lizard, then leaped at the flame demon. Astoria swung her longsword down, carving a diagonal wound into the enemy's chest. A viscous flame spurted out that I might have confused for blood.

The others made impressed noises. Maybe I had as well. I could sense the light of hope coming on in those who had almost succumbed to despair. Wouldn't Astoria be able to defeat this terrible monster?

But things wouldn't be so easy.

"It seems the miserable human has managed to wound me! That deserves a reward—take it!"

With a wrathful howl, the flame demon used both his longsword and his whip at once to launch a terrifically fierce offensive. It seemed he'd been vastly underestimating us—until Astoria's strike made him get serious.

The sword and whip flung all over the place, smashing into everything. The hall no longer had many safe spots. I yelled at the others to take refuge anywhere they could. Those able hid behind nearby doors.

The command seemed to draw the enemy's attention. The flame demon glanced at me, then looked back at Astoria.

"Knight. You act in that man's defense, do you? I see now. That man is your King, is he?"

What? Acting in my defense? Was this demon an idiot?

"I believe I would like to see the face of a Knight as the King she serves is killed in front of her. You there, man—do not move."

I flung myself away, and a moment later, the monster's fiery whip slashed the space where I'd been.

With no time to waste, I got up and started running. The lash swung down to crack at my feet, and as the embers licked at my back, he laughed loudly.

"Your King certainly knows how to scurry!"

I wasn't their King, but telling Balgor that wouldn't do me any good.

I let him chase me, running up the stairs at the edge of the hall. Walking and running were the hallmarks of a soldier. As I arrived at the top level, the demon smashed the stairs behind me. I kept on trying to flee, aiming for the upper-level walkway built along the wall. But then his whip flashed down in front of me, smashing the walkway to smithereens. I had stopped myself just in time, but my return path was already gone, too. With nowhere left to go, the flame demon laughed at me scornfully.

"Look, Knight. Your King is stranded."

"Sir Taiga!"

The flame demon didn't miss the opportunity created by Astoria's shout.

His lash cracked through the air and slammed into Snorts and Astoria from the side. Knight and rider were knocked away and slammed into the wall. Armor clanged against stone, and the blond woman cried in pain.

"Astoria!"

"And now it is over. I will reduce you to ash together."

The flame demon held its incandescent longsword aloft to strike me down.

And then a dagger, thrown from somewhere else, grazed his face.

"Hrrr...?"

The dagger bounced off his hard exterior and fell to the floor without leaving much of a scratch on him. It had been Troach, propped up with Mizuho's help.

It wasn't just the two of them, either. Even the subordinates, who were supposed to be finding safety from the flame demon's onslaught, started to creep out and hurled whatever spears or stones they could find. None of them seemed to do even a bit of actual damage, but the flames began to spurt from Balgor's body just a little bit harder. He was clearly annoyed.

"Know your place, scum!"

The blazing demon's enraged howl made the hall shake. Arrogant as he was, he couldn't tolerate the very fact that beings he saw as lesser were overcoming their fear to defy him. I knew the concept well, for humans thought the same way.

His whip cracked through the air, sending crimson sparks showering down on us. Seeing our subordinates yelping and scurrying for safety, the monster laughed.

"Sir Taiga! Sir Taiga!" Astoria was beckoning to me astride Snorts, which was struggling to stand back up. The young woman's armor had already been covered in scrapes and dents, but now it featured several new burn marks from the whip.

"Now's your chance! To me, quickly!"

May as well try!

I jumped off the edge of the walkway and landed on Snorts's back. I nearly slipped and fell off its scales, but I held on to the saddle's belt. The six-legged lizard gave an unhappy groan underneath me.

Though the flame demon had been preoccupied with tormenting the soldiers, he was not oblivious to what we were doing. His burning longsword was upon us in a flash. Thankfully, Snorts dodged in the nick of time.

The blade bit deeply into the wall, melting the stone and sending up smoke. When Balgor pulled his weapon free, the wall fractured, and the rock and sand it was built from collapsed heavily into the hall.

The flame demon fanned away the thick cloud of billowing dust with his whip. When our vision cleared, we saw that the entire upper wall of the hall's south side had completely caved in, connecting the hall to a cavern on the other side.

The flame demon peered through the dust and found us.

"Still alive? Persistent insects."

From atop the horse-lizard's back, I asked Astoria, "Can you move?"

"He got one of Snorts's legs…but we can still go!"

Astoria's own breath was ragged. With how hard she'd been hit, there was no way she could have been unscathed.

"Can you make it so he can't catch us?"

"I probably could… But are you telling me to flee?!" she demanded in disbelief.

Patiently, I answered, "Yes. If we don't draw him out of here, everyone will die."

"…I see. We're to be decoys, then?"

"I knew you'd understand."

"Right! In that case, Sir Taiga, make sure to record him chasing us!"

No sooner had she said that than she kicked Snorts in the sides. Twisting itself, Snorts began running up the slant created by the collapsed wall.

"Mizuho! Troach! Ignore us and withdraw!" I shouted.

The two of them burst out of their hiding place.

"Taiga, what do you mean to do?!"

"You have to be kidding! Wait—"

Behind us, as we burst into the new cavern on Snorts's back, the flame demon spread his wings.

"I will not allow you to escape!"

To see something so gigantic fly defied all reason. I watched in shock as the demon floated into the air, kicking up clouds of dust. He didn't take flight like a bird, instead levitating. He flapped his wings, chasing after us and landing in the cavern's entrance.

Snorts dashed through the natural cavern, which was filled with stalactites and stalagmites. It had tucked in its wounded middle-right leg, but the hooked claws on its other five grasped the earth, charging ahead with considerable speed. Behind us, the flame demon gave chase, breaking through stalactites as he went.

Good. At least we were able to draw him away from our allies.

But then Astoria gasped, realizing something. "Sir Taiga, I know this place!"

I realized it, too, a moment later. What a mistake. We'd fled right into the greatbat cave. I remembered the cave coming to a dead end when passing through it before. The cave-in was the only thing blocking it from the corridor wall!

If we continued this way, we'd arrive at the palace with an enraged demon of fire and flames on our tail. This was the worst mistake we could have made.

"What now, Sir Taiga?"

No side paths to detour through and no plan to hold him off if we stopped. If we failed here, he would be able to destroy the palace without opposition, and the others would be cut off from their return.

"Keep going. Just keep going," I replied. Astoria nodded.

Snorts dashed through the high-ceilinged passage and burst full-speed into the palace. Everyone who was standing there working gave cries of surprise. From the horse-lizard's back as it sprinted past the pillars, I yelled, "Everyone, retreat! Run away now! Hide yourselves!!"

Heavy footsteps rapidly approached. The flame demon appeared through the archway leading to the palace's northern passage. He stopped and looked around as the citizens screamed and fled.

"Oh? No wonder I felt this place was familiar. Why, this is my sacrificial altar!" the flame demon said, advancing at a leisurely pace. **"It was long ago, but I once had worshippers living in this area. They would throw their living sacrifices into this hall for me, and in exchange, I gave them flame. Though I do forget what happened to them in the end."**

I shuddered. The burn marks dotting this hall—those hadn't been traces of campfires. They were spots where this flame demon had once been offered ritual sacrifices!

"To come here of your own volition... How commendable. Yes, I do believe I have an idea. Miserable King and Knight, if you would

offer unto me one of you as a living sacrifice, I shall allow the other to live."

"I will not concede to your wicked machinations!" Astoria loudly called back.

The flame demon snorted. "I see. Then I will make your people deci—"

The demon's words came to an abrupt end when he beheld the scenery before him.

"...What—what is this?"

Even he seemed taken aback by the incredible sight of the Great Fracture. Monster or human, none in Million Dungeon were accustomed to such wide-open spaces.

Snorts stopped by the side of the flowing river. We could run farther by crawling along the cliffside, but we'd have to face our foe somewhere. This would probably be our last chance.

I alighted from the horse-lizard and gave the black mirror to Astoria.

"I'm returning this. Sorry, but I don't have any time to record. I'll draw him away."

"Sir Taiga, that is my job—"

"No, I'm better for it. I will create an opportunity, I promise. When I give the signal, you attack with everything you have."

"...All right."

I left Astoria and stood with the river to my back. Then, in a loud voice, I yelled to the flame demon.

"Hey, lumbering giant! Over here!"

"What's the matter? Couldn't wait your turn to be scorched to death?"

"More like I got tired of you standing there. You're in the way. So I decided to take you down."

"Take me down? Ha!" The flame demon regarded me with a sneer. "You don't even have a proper sword. What do you plan to do with that little stick?"

"Oh, this? Well, you see..."

I pointed the flashlight in my hand at his face and flipped the switch. Powerful light flooded his face.

Amid a bellowing roar, the monster covered his face with a hand.

"You wretch! What is that light?!"

His vision stolen, the demon howled in rage and blindly brought his whip down. The rocks on the dry riverbed crumbled and scattered upon impact. Fortunately, I was no longer among them. I'd withdrawn the moment his vision was gone.

As the flame demon attacked his surroundings wildly, he staggered toward the river, unsteady. The ends of his whip struck the water's surface, splashing up white vapor that rose upward.

I shouted, "Now, Astoria! Force him off!"

Snorts kicked off the ground and charged, delivering a full-force tackle to the enemy's back with all its speed and mass. It knocked the flame demon off his feet; he stumbled a step forward and fell into the river.

A plume of steam exploded into the air, and from within it came a deafening scream that reverberated throughout the Great Fracture. The water's flow as it fell to us from an upper stratum was quick—quick enough to wash away even the giant body of the flame demon. I watched closely as the river swallowed the monster. His hide changed to the gray of dead coals, cracked apart, and flaked off, exposing the burning fire within—whose heat was also extinguished...

And then it happened. From within the bubbling waves, something black and snakelike flew out and struck me hard. I froze up from the pain, and in an instant, it had wrapped around me and yanked me toward the river.

My head was submerged before I'd even had the chance to curse. As the raging current tossed me about, the flame demon's face suddenly appeared. Though his whitened, muddied eyes probably couldn't see anything anymore, I painfully felt his desire to take me down with him.

The whip, its flames put out, weakened and dissolved. However, I was already at the mercy of the surging current. With it going this fast, all the trash and driftwood became lethal weapons. When I tried to surface, something struck me in the head, and I immediately felt faint. Air began to leak from my lungs. The waterfall was right there, but I couldn't move. As I beheld the smile on the flame demon's face, moments before I tumbled to the basin far below, I passed out.

31

Someone was on the other side of the river. Two men stood there, looking at me. Neither of them was human above the shoulders.

One's head was that of an albino crow. The other's was a moray eel. It was the pair who had attacked me in the restroom in Haneda. They watched me, discussing something.

Hey, you. Were you the ones who brought me to this world? Why did you attack me? Explain yourselves...

I tried to speak, but for some reason, no words left my mouth, only water. I stopped, confused, but the liquid continued to bubble up. It surged out of my mouth and nose until I could no longer breathe. I dropped to my knees, then finally fell over to the side.

The pair shrugged, shook their heads, and turned their backs to me.

Wait... Don't run...

I reached out a hand before all went white.

32

Consciousness returned as the water was painfully expelled from my body.

"Taiga! Ahh, thank goodness!"

"Taiga, can you hear? Can you see me?"

Unable to respond to the disparate voices calling to me, I coughed up more liquid to the point where I thought my lungs were liable to come out.

When I finally lifted my face, I realized I was lying by the river, surrounded by everyone. I blinked.

"...What happened?"

"Astoria saved you from the river."

Troach pointed. I looked that way and saw Astoria, her armor soaking wet, leaning against Snorts and pointing the black mirror at me.

"If you want someone to thank, it's Snorts, not me. My mount was the one that jumped into the river, caught you in its mouth, and swam back to shore. Got that? Snorts."

"...Thank you, Snorts," I managed.

The wound-covered horse-lizard exhaled, not seeming very pleased.

"You weren't breathing, so we were all panicking."

"Yeah. We did our best to get you to spit up the water..."

Mizuho and Troach sat on the ground, looking drained.

"Thank you. Sorry for the scare."

"You're telling me..."

"I finally managed to lead everyone here, and you were on the verge of dying. I wasn't sure what to do."

"Well, wasn't that an incredible adventure? We defeated Balgor and saved everyone. Excellent, just excellent!" Astoria declared, the only one acting carefree.

"Get some good footage?" I asked the question sarcastically, but Astoria nodded, taking it seriously.

"Yeah. It was the best stream I've ever done."

"Glad to hear it. Sorry I couldn't record at the end. You were the highlight there, after all."

"You mean pushing the flame demon into the river? No need to worry. I got it all right here."

"How?" I inquired.

Astoria pointed to Snorts's saddle.

"There's a holder on the front of the saddle. If I put the mirror there, I can capture footage by myself. Everyone loves a first-person stream."

I sighed and looked up.

There may not have been any actual sky to be seen, but there was no ceiling here. And this day was, somehow, a little brighter. In addition to the glittering starlight on the walls, a faint light was shining on us from higher up in the Great Fracture.

All cried out, "Hurrah! Three cheers for the Great Camp Bravo Kingdom!"

As I listened to their voices echo through the massive fissure, a peculiar thought came to mind.

...I want to drink some tea. Some nice, warm, real tea.

Still, no matter how hard I wished for it, tea leaves wouldn't appear from nowhere as if by magic, and I remained forsaken and soaking wet. Resting on my laurels wouldn't do. There were people who needed me. In that sense, maybe the situation was even worse now than it had been when I'd first arrived in Million Dungeon.

Sighing, I got to my feet. It looked like I'd have to rough it in this world a while longer—until I happened across some tea, at least.

Afterword

Hello, this is Iori Miyazawa. I'm the author.

This novel was based on the campaign setting of a tabletop RPG called *Labyrinth Kingdom*. It's an original transported-to-another-world, or *isekai*, story. The protagonist is a thirty-something half-Japanese, half-British man who was discharged from the Special Air Service.

Not knowing the source material or about special-forces teams shouldn't be a problem. You don't have to be familiar with anything from the game or be well versed in military matters—you should still be able to read it and find it interesting.

The SAS, to which the main character Taiga Andou-Garrett belonged, is a UK fighting force said to be the best in the world. They train at a high level and have an abundance of combat experience. The entrance exams are horrifically brutal, and even those who fail are respected simply for making an attempt.

Our protagonist served with the SAS for twenty years; he's had a whole lot drilled into him. I envisioned a sternly handsome sort of man, like the British actors Tom Hardy, Daniel Craig, and James McAvoy, when creating him.

Being a former SAS member who is half-Japanese and half-British, he may immediately remind many people of the protagonist in the famous manga *Master Keaton*, Taichi Hiraga-Keaton. I loved the author as well. (The names sounding somewhat similar was coincidental, though, not on purpose.)

Labyrinth Kingdom takes place in what used to be a totally normal fantasy world, the kind you've all probably seen in video games and *isekai* stories before. But then a magical disaster called the Dungeon Calamity occurred, and a maze swallowed up the world.

The "totally normal" fantasy setting was engulfed in darkness, transformed into a hell with no exit.

The dungeon itself expands both aboveground and below, forming countless layers. Even the ocean and sky have been incorporated into it.

Humans were scattered throughout this world, now known as Million Dungeon, and they created small, huddled kingdoms with populations in the dozens. To obtain food and resources, they need to set foot into unexplored areas of the labyrinth. They have to expand their nation's territory by venturing into a place filled with monsters and traps around every corner. In the original tabletop RPG, the players control the Landmakers leading one of those small countries.

Our main character, Taiga, is suddenly thrown into that harsh world and ends up a Landmaker himself. Being a former special-forces soldier, Taiga is very skilled in survival techniques, but it's still not easy for him to endure in this strange world that's so different from the Earth he knows. Things only get more difficult as he's forced to protect others, too. Will Taiga be able to safeguard these people and save his fledgling nation from utter destruction? This story is sort of like the hard-mode version of an *isekai* and civilization manager.

Labyrinth Kingdom first debuted in 2004. Toichiro Kawashima of Adventure Planning Service designed the game. He and a manga-ka named Rasenjin Hayami each wrote about half the world's backstory. Many other writers contributed to it after that, and every once in a while, a new one is added to renew and continue things. With such a rich history, I personally had a lot of interest in the title, so I'm happy to have been blessed with the opportunity to create a novel in this setting.

Since 2004, *Labyrinth Kingdom* has undergone several versions. Most recently, in 2018, Kadokawa released it in the form of the *Labyrinth Kingdom Basic Rule Book*. The game has enjoyed long-lived popularity.

To conclude, I'd like to offer my gratitude to a few people. Thank you to everyone involved in the production of *Labyrinth Kingdom* and all the players who love the game. My sincerest appreciation to all involved with this novel, especially Yo Shimizu, who drew the beautiful illustrations. But most of all, I want to thank you for picking up this book.